Martínez, Marcelo Ariel
The butterfly café and other fantastic stories / Marcelo Ariel
Martínez – 1st edition.
166 p. ; 15,24 x 22,86 cm.

© 2021, Marcelo Ariel Martínez.
First Edition. All rights reserved.
© Identification Safe Creative: **2307314938646**
ISBN: **9798854445986**

E-mail:
marcemartinezinfo@gmail.com
Instagram: @marcemartinezescritor
Ilustration: Mercedes Laserna – m.laserna.dg@gmail.com
Translation: Jennifer Woodley – jwoodley@ilivelanguages.com

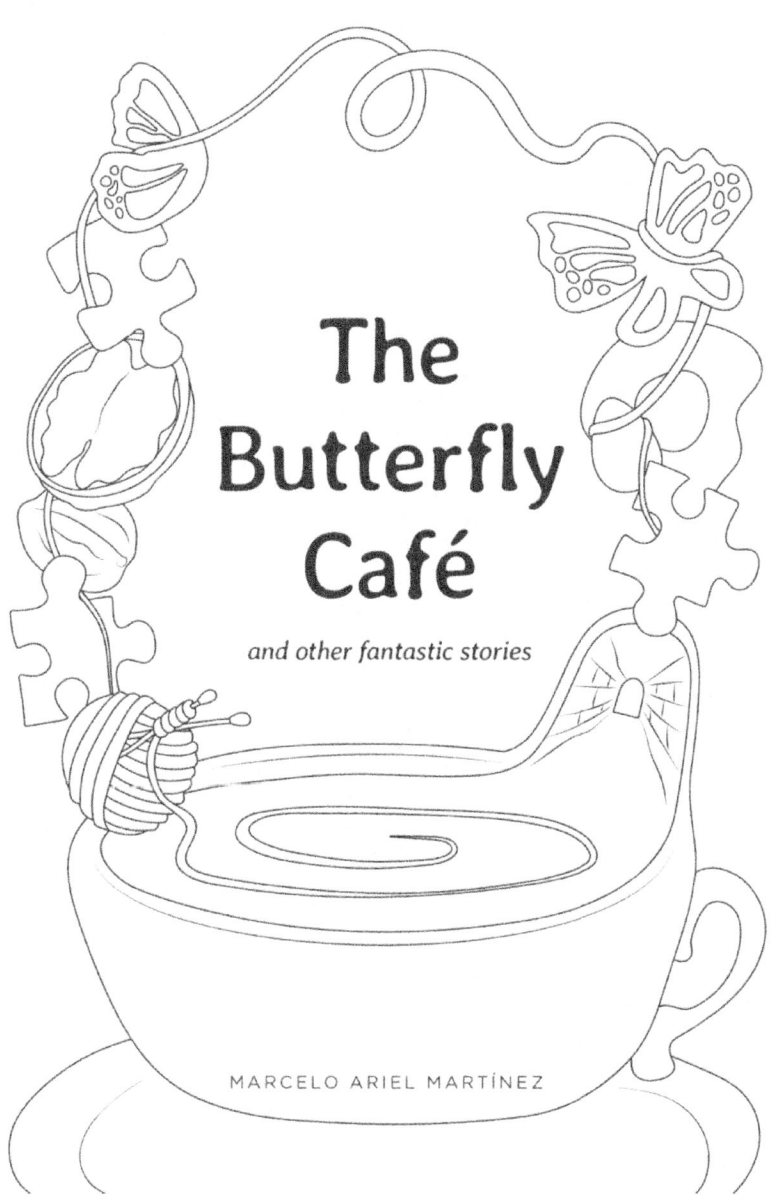

The Butterfly Café

and other fantastic stories

MARCELO ARIEL MARTÍNEZ

Index

The butterfly café

The sweater

Walnuts

A kiss on the forehead

Omelette

Trouble dying

Prologue

There are paths we walk alone. Others, we make accompanied. They all help us to get to know each other a little better, and even more so when we pay attention to the road.

Opening up is giving us the chance to get to know each other, it is being vulnerable to everything that happens around us; it is allowing the senses to capture what is happening on every isde of us and letting our body be that sponge which absorbs and then, when constricted, squeezes it all. It's that constant back and forth that feeds us back.

This path begins by opening the door of a very particular café, then sheltering you in a warm coat of love. It will then twist your mind like the walnut tree does when it grows and it will kiss your forehead to transport yourself within you and plant a precious seed of nostalgia. The ship will sail from there in shock and anchor at the door of a family full of love. Finally, the end: you will see the light at the end of the tunnel through Martha's eyes and you will want to enjoy all of these stories again, opening the door of the Café de las Mariposas, consciously entering an infinite loop of love, fantasy and humour.

May you enjoy the tour as many times as you wish!

Just turn the page and open the door...

Sincerely,
Marcelo A. Martínez

The butterfly Café

•

*Thank you for teaching me
so much. Thank you for
allowing me to learn from
you. Thank you for being
eternal, my friend.*

It needs to be noted that modern tales don't start with '*Once upon a time...*' anymore, which belongs to an era in which dragons, leprechauns, elves and wizards lived among people. However, mine cannot be told without that introduction to legends, because the who saved me was one of *them...*

Once upon a time there was a woman who had heard the rumor about the existence of a butterfly so big, so big, that with her wings, immense as those of a condor, and as colorful as a clown's costume, could embrace life entirely and give color to sadness. The woman also heard about *The Butterfly Café*, located in a corner of the city. It was said that that was the home of the great butterfly, and that the butterflies which flew all around while you were having coffee were her own daughters and hence, they spread out some of her magic. It was said that those people who entered the café came out differently, changed, content, happy, stronger…

The woman had woken up a bit sad that morning, so she decided to go that day to the café to verify the truth of the rumor. When she arrived, she could feel the magic even before going in. She stood at the door in awe, contemplating it jaw-dropped, sunk in a relaxing music that came from the inside. Secured between old and powerful carob wood posts was a butterfly-shaped glass frame; the wings were made of little stained glass window of all the colors in the galaxy, which reflected symmetrically on the opposite side as if it were its mirror.

The woman pushed the door softly, and immediately, the scent – a mixture of Costa Rican coffee grains and lavender from field tenderly moist with dew– gently embraced her chest, as morning mist leaving the bare feet exposed. Braids of wicker, a bit linger than the height of the door, dropped as curtains to prevent the butterflies from fleeing the premises. Once through them, her pupils glowed as stars on a clear night, and they pressed over the corners of her mouth drawing a wide smile: butterflies of all sizes and colors flew all over and around.

A man wearing a white shirt with a pattern of butterflies in various pastel colors approached her and, with a friendly smile, invited her to take a seat. He walked her in and gave her a menu, which was shaped as a butterfly, indeed. He then walked away.

The woman observed the place in such an amazement that every detail was engraved in her eyes as a tattoo is on the skin. However, it was the intrinsic details the ones that she absorbed in the way of a sponge forgotten in the bathtub would. The atmosphere and its flawless ferocity in the calm and happiness extrapolated to people were unbelievable. It was impeccable the way in which each butterfly that landed on somebody would make them smile, just as a magician takes a rabbit from his top-hat.

Breakfast was wonderful with all the butterflies around. Many landed on her and made her forget the sadness she had woken up feeling. She noted that one of them was taking off from her shoulder like a plane taxing on a runway, it escaped though a corridor and disappeared out of her sight.

The following day, the woman woke up once again feeling the same sadness and she told herself that she would take breakfast at The Butterfly Café. It had felt good, why shouldn't she do it again? The previous day had been wonderful after the café with all the butterflies flying all around her. She felt the need to restore her energies to face the day. So, she git dressed, put on some makeup and went out.

At the café, more butterflies than the day before approached her and made her feel happier that ever, maybe because the sugar bowl was open. She noticed once more that all the butterflies that flew away from her, went down the same corridor as those the day before had gone. She found it curious, but didn't consider it really important. At a moment, she stood and went to the toilet. When she looked in the mirror, she saw herself more beautiful, more radiant, more colorful, as if the makeup she had put on in the morning had had a delayed effect. She perceived herself more alive, more attractive, O-VER-WEL-MING.

After the café, it was a splendid morning. The rest of the day as well, indeed. She had come out head up, shoulders wide and chest up front, like a horse parading. The high-heeled shoes stroke clip-clop, clip-clop as metal hooves on the pavement. It was her against the world.

When night set in, the woman started to feel a slight sensation of sadness, which clearly grew on the following morning; that is why once she got up and looked in the mirror, she noticed herself a bit pale, as if her blood pressure had dropped, so she put on some makeup to counteract her aspect. However, whether she smeared her face or wore any ornament she could put on, she could not hide from her emotions. She could do it as a pose, she could pretend before the cheerless, expectation lacking gaze of passersby. Yet, she could not hide from herself. However, that's what the butterflies were for…

The woman returned to the café that morning, to fill herself with joy, with energy to face the day. Upon sitting at the table, many butterflies came close to her, many more than the previous day; and the woman had the feeling that several of them had known her all her life and were coming to greet her. They hovered around for a while and then disappeared though the same corridor as usual. At a moment, while she was lifting the cup of tea to reach her mouth, she realized that a little butterfly had landed on that same hand she was holding the cup with. She attentively observed it and was filled with awe when she saw that the butterfly's wings were becoming colorless and her hand took on a livelier tonality. Immediately after it turned black and white, the insect flew through the same corridor as all the others. Then, the woman paid more attention to the butterflies that surrounded her and noticed, in great amazement, that those that flew away showed a gray monochrome, while those that emerged from the corridor carried colors.

The next morning, there was no makeup that could conceal how she felt. She dragged sadness and sorrow as anchors. The woman got up, looked in the mirror and didn't believe she was actually that person the mirror was reflecting. She was as pale as a corpse. She put on makeup, yes. By the means she could. But she needed the butterflies. She needed *them*.

She walked into the bar and it was not necessary to tell the waiter she was going to order coffee.

- "The usual?," he asked.
- "The usual," she answered.

The butterflies came on to her as a bee hive protecting their queen, as if she was really their queen. They didn't attack her, not at all; but it was a kind of impenetrable cloud of butterflies what she had over her head. Suddenly, the woman seemed to have taken all the butterflies at the café in a selfish though not predetermined way: she didn't want them all with her, but they were there. Was it, maybe, that the woman was releasing some sort of pheromone related to the fact of feeling that she needed them? Was it possibly that the butterflies perceived that need and went towards her to cheer her day up, to take her sadness away? Perhaps, her feelings allowed the release of substances to the exterior that called the attention of those insects? All the people at the place observed the situation with amazement.

However, from one moment to another, a butterfly fell into the woman's coffee. Dead. Colorless and dead. And it was followed by other a few seconds later, to the sides of the cup. Then, an uproar could be heard around, which blended in with a deep choked cry of surprise and anguish. The woman lifted her head and looked. Many butterflies flying towards the corridor were fainting and plunging, stiff. They dropped like missiles, everywhere.

The woman felt overwhelmed with shame when she realized that all the butterflies that were dying were all of those that had approached to share their bliss with her. She tried, then, to shoo away the ones that were still around her: she waved her hands, shook her head, her body, but got no results: the butterflies stayed there. She dropped to the floor to pick up those that were already dead. She didn't know what she would do with them, she knew she could not save them, however…however, while she did that, she apologized. Until she got up suddenly and started running desperately, with tears in her eyes, without saying a word. She stopped for a second in front of the counter, left a high-denomination bill and didn't wait for the change. She didn't want it. She ran away.

The following morning was the worst of all. The woman woke up colorless and there was no makeup to disguise the tremendous grief she was carrying on her. Even if her lipstick was of crimson red, when she pressed it against and ran it along her mouth, her lips stayed white. Nothing had colors. Not her skin, nor her hair. Nor her eyes or her inner organs. Not her blood nor her thoughts. She was like a character taken out of the earliest television, around the 1920s, and place din the middle of a colorful jungle in the new millennium. She felt out of place and came to point at which she went crazy. Everything around her had colors, but not her.

She tried a thousand and one ways of getting some color to blend with the world around her: she wore eyeshadow, she polished her nails, she used self-tanning cream on her body, she changed her lipstick...even when she noticed that her lips wouldn't take on any color, she used it all over her face, in an abstract way. However, nothing happened. Absolutely nothing was working. Desperate, she went to the kitchen, open a tomato sauce can and poured it on herself, and all the same, when the sauce touched her body, the color disappeared, and the woman remained of that monochrome tonality. She burst into tears uncontrollably, kneeling on the kitchen floor, without dropping the tomato sauce can.

She felt then that something had touched her hand. She opened her eyes and saw a colorful butterfly lying on her. She didn't know how it had got in but it was there.

She calmed her crying and her distressed sighs while she observed it slowly open and close its wings. Strangely, it didn't share its color with her as the others had done at the café on the previous days. It simply stayed there, resting ion her hand, showing its colors to her. The woman interpreted that as an invitation to the café, although she quickly nodded her head to refuse and shook her hand trying to make fly away; after what had happened the day before, she wouldn't go back to the café for something like that - or worse- to happen again because of her. Nevertheless, the butterfly didn't leave. Even if she tried a thousand times to shoo it away, it would take off and fly around, make a U turn in the air and return. Finally, the woman quit waving her hand and accepted the said invitation when the insect landed and once again opened its wings slowly showing its colors.

The woman arrived at the café. As she went in, everyone's eyes were fixed on her. Then, she her the murmur about her monochrome aspect. She noticed how the waiter pretended to hide his surprise while he invited her to get a seat at one of the tables. No sooner had she sat, that all, absolutely all the butterflies in the place came on to her as a pack of starving hyenas going after a prey left behind by a group of lionesses.

The woman clearly felt frightened, essentially when she realized that the butterflies had not only set on her shoulders and back, but they were holding as tight as if they had rapacious claws; it then when they fluttered all together, and lifted her feet from the ground.

The butterflies flew the woman to the corridor where they would disappear every time they passed their colors on to someone. They went in there with her, into the twilight, until they reached a sort of greenhouse full of plants and other butterflies in a significant number. The butterflies left her there in the greenhouse and returned to where they had come from. The woman turned her head to watch them and noticed that the café was no longer in sight. The woman never knew if the insects had flown her in a straight line through a very looooooooong tunnel, if they had made a turn at some point, if they had gone down some steps or if they simply and marvelously had crossed some kind of magical portal.

The woman contemplated the place jaw-dropped. She didn't understand how it was possible for such a greenhouse to be there, erected as an underworld which seemed to be endless, both in width and in length; she looked up and it seemed to be endless also in height. She wasn't interested in knowing, anyway. She would rather feel captivated by the magic it transmitted; and, in case she was still asleep, enjoy such a splendid dream. However, what was curious about the whole situation was that in front of her there was a very elegant, white, steel, garden table and two chairs: fancy, white, for the garden, made of steel. Behind the table, hanging peacefully from the thick branch of an old tree, there was a giant cocoon, which a few seconds later started to move and crack. From inside, some fingers emerged, followed by a hand and an arm. Then appeared a foot, a leg, another foot and another leg. Thus, little by little, the cocoon opened and from it a woman lent out. She was beautiful. She was naked and under one of her breasts, the woman noticed she had a small scar. She had a mole on one side of her slightly snubbed nose and straight hair- shyly tangled- fell down over her shoulders with its wildish ends. She had a gorgeous smile and the sheer act of looking at her transmitted…it transmitted peace. And all of a sudden, standing there with her eyes still shut, with a pose similar to that of *The Vitruvian Man* of Da Vinci, but with her hands to the sides of her body, a pair of gigantic wings unfolded and opened behind her, displaying an endless color palette together with the glow and the attractiveness of a peacock's tail.

The instant she opened her wings, innumerable little butterflies, which seemed to be sheltering under them, flew away to the woman and they elevated forming a kind of cone until each drew the trajectory of the desired flight. Then, she took a deep breath through the nose, and held the air in for some seconds; she exhaled slowly, and opened her eyes: they were light brown and they shone glitteringly.

The human butterfly greeted the woman by waving her hand in the air, however, the woman was unable to react. The woman was absolutely astonished. Even more so when eight butterflies appeared next around the human butterfly- four on each side- and flew carrying two tea cups and left them on the table. Consecutively, the human butterfly wrapped herself in her enormous wings and, when she opened them again, she was wearing a pink sleeveless shirt and a long skirt of pastel yellow with fine red and orange lines. With a gesture of her hand, she invited the woman to take a seat and walked towards the table to join her for coffee.

The woman took some time to respond but accepted the invitation: she approached the table and sat.

"What's your name?" asked the human butterfly, grabbing the cup and crossing her legs.

"S-Sa-Sandra," she stuttered

"What a color you have, Sandra!" The human butterfly exclaimed, contemplating her from top to bottom. "Truth be told, you have no color! What's happening to you?"

Sandra didn't know what to answer. She shrugged. She didn't know what was happening to her, why she was sad…So she just replied:

"I'm sad."

"That I already know. My question was not '*How are you*' but '*What's happening to you?*'", and looked at her right in the eyes.

The woman felt the pupils of the human butterfly digging into hers as a dagger, very intense. It was as if she wanted to dig into her soul, so subtly and thoroughly as a paleontologist would do with a dinosaur bone, using a toothbrush to reach the most important detail that would allow him to determine which dinosaur such a bone belonged to.

Then, Sandra slightly leapt off her seat when the human butterfly opened her extremities suddenly and abruptly; some of her coffee was spilled. The butterfly wrapped the conversation space around with her wings. Sandra watched, in wonder, how such extremities enclosed her through her back and formed a much more private and intimate space among her, the butterfly, the table, the chairs and the two cups of coffee. Nothing nor nobody else. Not even the small butterflies that were hovering around dared enter the circle.

"You can go naked," said the butterfly.

Sandra looked to one side. To the other. She looked her in the eyes and blinked in confusion. *"To get naked?" she wondered.*

The butterfly took her cup of coffee without taking her eyes away from her. She sipped and made a little noise. She left the cup on the table again and said:

"Get naked."

Sandra looked around again. No one was looking. It was only her and the human butterfly. She didn't understand why the latter was asking her to get naked. In some way, she felt a little embarrassed, however, the woman seemed trustworthy, so after a few seconds of hesitation, she decided to do it. She stood up and when she made the first attempt at taking something off, the woman stopped her:

"You don't need to take your clothes of."

"But..," Sandra felt confused.

"Get naked," the woman insisted, with a sharp, compact and crystalline look, slightly leaning her head, "get naked of what covers your soul; take the shell off; take off your makeup. Tell me, especially, tell yourself, listen to yourself, feel yourself: what is happening to you, what do you feel, why is it that you have no color, why you are sad. Get naked. Pull that thread that hangs from your shirt. Pull, pull, pull, until your breasts are out, because our breasts are sacred, aren't they? Who wouldn't be proud if her breasts? Food to the helpless, a symbol of giving life, of giving color to…" and she let out a giggle, "to the feeling that start to build, right? Such as love. The look among mother and child while this is clinging to its nipple. How crazy is that!" she let out another giggle similar to the previous one, this time together with a little shrug, "How powerful! The most powerful of all feelings, don't you think? So," she took a deep breath and exhaled, "I repeat: *who wouldn't be proud of her breasts?"*

"Look!" she exclaimed, suddenly lifting her shirt and showing the woman a scar right below one of her breasts, "you surely have already noted: here is a symbol of love...of love and struggle," she pulled her shirt down. "And love is who saves you: it allows you to talk to yourself, to understand yourself, to assimilate yourself, to accept and listen to yourself, to love and feel yourself...," she made a pause to take another sip of coffee. When she put the cup down, she repeated: "Take a seat, please. Have some coffee and get naked. Get naked to the boobs!"

Sandra's eyes were flooded in silence while she heard the butterfly speaking. She cleaned her face as she could, nervously, with her fingers. She slowly sat down, she was trembling; she noticed that her legs had loosened. She became aware then that a white light was growing increasingly intense around her until it became incandescent; it was coming from the inside of the butterfly's wings, they were radiating it themselves.

"It will be you yourself who will make color return to your life, woman," the butterfly added. "It won't be me. I will only help you get naked. Can you see the light? It's only white light. I understand that you know about its fragmentation in colors, right? Well then, the more naked you get, the more the light will filter through you and the more colors will be seen fragmented. Look at that gray tonality of sadness that you are carrying, please! I'm not the one to cure you, nor my butterflies giving you their colors! It's you, yourself, of course! So, take the light and make it into colors! Create your own colors! Paint yourself! But not in appearance! Stop wearing that makeup! Paint yourself in the inside! Get naked!"

Sandra took a deep breath and got comfortable in her seat. She approached the cup of coffee, took it and moved towards her chest, nesting it in her hand. She took a drink and started to perceive the light around her as a warm hug which, little by little, in spite of not having said one word yet, had initiated a process of radiation of colors inside itself. She felt a small ball in her belly, somewhere around her belly-button, as if it was an entrance door to her soul. She perceived some kind on connection of the umbilical type, as if she was once again connected to her mother inside her womb. The light was entering through there like food during her gestation. It was nurturing her. It was giving her life, colors. It was painting her.

"All that about the butterflies in your stomach when you're in love," the butterfly added, "well, it is true!" she laughed. "When you are in love with yourself, of course! And that's because you feel certain about taking the next step! Being happy! You can't be happy if you don't love yourself!"

Then, Sandra started talking. She talked to herself, aloud in order to hear, to feel the vibration of her voice on her skin. She talked to herself about what was happening to her. When she got stuck, the butterfly asked her questions to allow her to unravel, and continue pulling from the thread. Little by little her body was recovering its color.

At a moment, the light went out and the butterfly put her wings back in their place, behind her back. She made herself comfortable in her seat with her shoulders spread, legs crossed and the cup of coffee on her hand to the height of her smiling lips. She looked at the woman in front of her, who didn't stop looking at herself, she didn't stop looking at the beautiful colors her being had at that moment. She was shedding tears of joy. She was laughing. She laughing and crying. Unexpectedly, she stood up and jumped on to the butterfly giving her a hug so tight and powerful that it made the butterfly also shed a tear of joy.

"When I have a daughter, I will name her after you!", Sandra thanked, looking intensely in the eyes of the butterfly, while she wiped hers. "By the way, what's your name?"

"Leticia."

"Leticia *Butterfly*!", the woman smiled. "How much do I owe you!?"

"Nothing, woman. Just stop killing my butterflies when you come over to the café to have a cup of coffee," she said ironically, letting put a grin.

"I'm terribly sorry fo that, " the woman apologized regretfully. "What can I do to..."

"Nothing," the butterfly interrupted her with a hand in the air. "You don't owe me anything! Love yourself! Simply love yourself! And if a need a little light boost, come and see me!" she smiled and hugged her tight.

Sandra returned the hug. She turned and headed for the door. However, the woman butterfly interrupted her before she was gone, so she was forced to turn around:

"By the way! I like it more in Italian!"

Sandra looked at her in disconcert. She didn't understand what she was talking about. And the butterfly woman, noticing her bewildered expression, explained:

"Butterfly. I like more the word *butterfly* in Italian."

"So… Leticia?"

"Farfalla. Leticia *Farfalla*," she said extending her arms and wings happily, showing all, absolutely all of her colors.

Sandra gave her back an enormous grin.

After that day, I only saw her once…when my daughter was born. I came to the café and went in with my pushchair. The butterflies leapt onto me that day, quite like they had done some time before when they saw me in black and white. But this time they didn't drop dead or anything of the kind. On the contrary, they laid on me and they were filled with colors. They took me to their master, their creator. And there, for the first time, both Leticias looked at each other in the eyes.

Today, ten years after that encounter, my daughter has come to tell me she has woken up with a terrible and strange pain on her back. When I lifted her shirt, I could see how two butterfly wings were emerging from her…

The sweater

•

The darkness grew little by little. The chilling night came along with fierce gulps of air. *Lucky!* Old Mrs. Bretwon laid comfortably in the orange armchair by the lighted fireplace, knitting a sweater for her seven-year-old granddaughter.

The wood was turned into charcoal and then turned into ashes. The great tongues of fire danced and lightly devoured the dried wood, keeping the house warm. Mrs. Bretwon had to stop knittingfor a short time to add more fuel to the fire.

She got up from her seat and took three to four steps. Gripping a piece of lightweight log with both hands, she turned toward the fire and threw it there. She sat down again in the comfortable chair, took the sweater -which, previously, she had left resting on its arm- and continued with the knitting.

The smoke caused by the fire –which was burning the new log with enthusiasm-, ran through the chimney of the small fireplace towards the outside, where its particles would spread, trying to occupy most of the atmosphere.

The strong winds were accompanied by a great rainstorm. Gray clouds covered the sky followed by lightning, and thena thunder. Soon, it started to rain.

The old woman turned her gaze to the window. She was afraid. The water -in the form of enormous drops- collided against it, causing a loud and terrifying noise.

She got up from the chair again, putting her sweater on the armrest, along with the knitting needles and the pink ball of wool. Slowly, she crossed the living room, turned on a corridor light, took two steps, and turned to her right. She made light pressure on a switch on the wall. The kitchen lit up.

She took a cup from the cupboard and put a linden tea bag inside. She took the box of matches and took one of them out. She lit it up and walked over to the stove. She opened the gas to the lower left burner and, with the match still lit, brought it closer. Once lit, she took a container and loaded it with water. She put it to heat.

She went to the armchair to finish her granddaughter's sweater while she waited for the water to heat up. She crossed the living room again to sit in the comfortable seat. She took up the knitting needles again and continued knitting.

Old Mrs. Bretwon was knitting non-stop, trying to finish her granddaughter's sweater before she arrived and she had not noticed that the fire in the hearth was slowly disappearing. At any moment, she would arrive with her parents and the birthday present would not be ready for the girl.

This would be the right moment to give it to her since she had been promising it every night, in every dream...

Done. Thank God!, she thought.

The doorbell rang. The old woman left the sweater on the armrest of the chair. She got up from the seat, crossed the living room once more, and headed to the hall. She walked to the front door and put her hand on the doorknob.

The girl turned the knob, opened the door, and quickly entered the warm and comfortable house. The parents did something similar. They took off the raining coats and hung them on a carob tree rack.

The girl ran into the living room to try to light the fireplace on. Upon arrival, she observed that something red glowed among the ashes: someone had lit the fire up. She thought of her mother. She always did it: she would turn it on to keep the house warm during the winter season, when they were away.

She turned her gaze to the orange chair. A sweater. The sweater that her grandmother had dreamt of knitting for her. Since the old woman passed away the day she was born, she only knew her from photos and she appeared to her every night, in each of her dreams, holding that pink sweater.

The only way to confirm the uncertain, the unbelievable, was to go to the kitchen. And there they were: the water in the container would be boiling and the linden tea bag, inside a cup ... Just as her grandmother had promised her the night before.

Walnuts

•

To my GREAT FRIEND ONDŘEJ

Ondřej was smoking his morning cigarette at the long porch shaped as a terrace, looking at the treetops in the forest that displayed itself with a beautiful green luxuriance across his house's fence. He was wearing his blue robe, slippers and the hand that was not holding the cigarette was lying under the opposite armpit, with the arm crossed.

He lived in Svatá, a small village at the top of the hill in the outskirts of Beroun. A city located around 50 kilometers from Prague. His house was absolutely cozy, surrounded by a pretty garden. It had different kinds of pine trees and some bushes also perennial, and an impressive walnut tree; Ondřej's look fixed on the latter.

He turned and saw his grandmother sitting in the bench they had in a corner and he noticed she was also looking at the walnut tree. He approached and sat next to her.

"Do you think it's OK there?" he asked her and pointed to the walnut tree with the hand that held the cigarette.

She nodded in affirmation and he hugged her with an arm, crossing it behind her back, and grabbing her opposite shoulder firmly. She left her head gently drop over his shoulder and breathed deeply. Ondřej felt the vibration of his grandmother's body when inhaling and exhaling. He noticed the deep dismay she felt inside and did not wish to express. It was there that his fingers pressed more intensely his grandma's shoulder and let out:

"We'll do it together after lunch, do not worry."

She nodded again, without uttering a word. She closed her eyes and rested on his shoulder.

After lunch, Ondřej went behind the house to the shed where they kept the tools and took a shovel. He walked with it towards the walnut tree, where his grandma was already waiting, with his grandfather's ashes sheltered inside a ceramic container. She looked at the walnut tree, from the foot to the leaves, with a calmed, still intensity and deep temperance. She gave a wince when Ondřej, already by her side, put his hand on her shoulder.

The young man started digging at the foot of the walnut tree, his grandmother stopped him:

"Ondřej, don't dig a hole."

He looked at her in surprise.

"I have a better idea...Why don't you make a channel around the trunk, please? –she asked. "You know this walnut tree was your grandfather's favorite and I would like..." she tried not to cry. She gulped inwardly and continued: "I would like you to make a small furrow around the trunk. I will scatter his ashes around it so that he protects it..." she stopped, made a pause to gulp again and bite her lips; this time, she sobbed softly, "so that he protects it..." she repeated, looking at her grandson right into the eyes y they went watery "...forever, so that he embraces it forever", and she shed a tear that rolled down her cheek all the way to her chin. Then two other tears followed: one from the other eye, and one from the same, which followed the same path as the first one.

Ondřej left the shovel aside and hugged her tightly against his chest. Then he pushed her away, kissed her in her forehead and started doing what she asked for.

The following days, Ondřej found, every morning, his grandmother watering all around the walnut tree. She did it with a watering can that spread drops softly and gently on the ground, allowing for their complete absorption. There wasn't a morning she didn't do that, except when it rained. She didn't pour too much water, either; no! No! Just a little, like a caress to her late husband.

Ondřej, meanwhile, observed her every morning from the porch that he had as a terrace, just awoken, her blue robe on, and smoking his cigarette with one of his arms crossed over the other. When he saw that his grandma was done watering, he would go inside and heat the kettle to make her come coffee. He, however, would prepare himself some *mate,* a custom he had acquired from his great Argentinian friend, with whom he ended up feeling just as brother.

The mornings during the spring and the summer continued to be quite dreary. Jerry – a small and somewhat restless dog, without a determined breed, and coming into his teenage years – had joined the family to bring a little more company and joy, and why not, some trouble in the garden -like when he had unburied all the tomato plants. However, he had never got within a meter from the walnut tree, even when the ground around there was softer than that of the little orchard at the back.

When the Autumn arrived, the walnuts fell and the lady harvested them, collecting them from the ground and putting them in glass jars. Ondřej took down those that were still hanging from the branches with the help of one of his brothers - his Argentinian friend-, a ladder and a couple of broom sticks. With a couple of knocks, the walnuts would fall like sharp riffles to the head; and it did hurt if they got your head! *Do prdelé!,* Ondřej could be heard saying quite often, every time that one of the fruits hit him at the union of the parietal bones.

With part of the collected walnuts, the woman made a cake. The remainder was successfully sold the following day at the local market of the town.

The next morning was as any other. Although the night had been different: the young man had dreamed of his grandfather. Clearly, the talk he had the day before with his grandma about him and everything the walnut tree meant to him had affected him.

Ondřej had woken up that morning feeling a bit nostalgic, but fine. He lit his cigarette in the porch, while he observed his grandma watering the walnut tree and Jerry was running around and hopping trying to get attention. He would bring some lost toy or stick to Ondřej's feet and he would throw it away again for him to go fetch it.

Then, his grandma asked him to make her some coffee. Ondřej nodded, taking a last puff at the cigarette and putting it down on the wooden handrail that separated the porch from the garden. He had focused his look on how the ashes crammed against one another; and played briefly with them. After that, he looked up and turned towards the kitchen; however, he stopped for a second and turned back to the street. He thought he had seen his grandfather walking by. It was fleeting. He was thoughtful for a moment. Immediately, he shook his head, like a dog shaking away the wet, as he tried to remove that melancholic thought and he went to the kitchen to make coffee for his grandma.

They had their coffee inside the house, while they talked about the next plants the lady wanted to set in the garden and they agreed to go to the nursery in the afternoon. Also, the lady made a short list of the things she needed then to make lunch, since her daughter - Ondřej's mother- and her other grandchildren were coming to the house. It wasn't necessary to go to the supermarket in the outskirts of the town; the shop three blocks away from house would have everything, but the lady couldn't walk too much, that's why she had asked Ondřej to get them.

The young man finished the coffee, took Jerry's leash and headed with the dog for the little shop, and they would take the chance of going for a walk in the forest on their way. There was almost no one walking in the lushness of the woods. However, he confused the few people he could see in the distance with his grandfather; and he had to shake his head, blink and rub his eyes several times.

Once at the shop, he tied Jerry outside. He petted his head and told him to be good and that he would be back. He searched in his pockets for the shopping list his grandma had given him, and a voice, after the bell that rang upon the opening and closing of the door, kindly saying "*Dobrý den*" forced him to look up and greet as well. He wasn't even able to finish the first word:

"*Dob...*"

The voice of that person had made him think. And when he lifted his head, he had to rub his eyes once again and wipe his glasses, since he didn't know if what he thought he was seeing was in fact what he saw.

The voice had been as clear as his grandpa's and when he looked up, he thought he had seen the back of his grandfather's head, however, by the time he put his glasses on, the person was already gone.

He entered the shop and he was alone. He picked up the items in the list and paid. It appeared strange to him that the shop assistant was a young man, who looked particularly familiar to him. Generally, the cashier was a woman. It was probable that they had hired someone new. He greeted kindly and asked him if he was new and, before the assistant answered, he went ahead inquiring about how long he had been working there. The assistant looked at him in surprise, while he gave Ondřej the change and stated that he had always worked there. That he had always been at the cashier. Ondřej felt puzzled. He apologized - with a noticeable shade of embarrassment in his voice- and he left the store thinking whether the woman had had a surgical change of sex or had gone into some treatment related to that and he told himself that he would keep his mouth shut next time.

When he arrived back home, he noticed his grandmother was submerged in a nostalgic atmosphere, contemplating old family photographs, and basically photos of his grandfather. He insisted to please put the photos away, because it was no doing her any good to have grandpa so much in mind, and so intensely. He recommended that for her, but also - even if he didn't clarify it - because all this was starting to affect him in a wild way. What's more, in a glimpse in one of the photographs while he helped his grandma put them away, he even thought he had seen the young man who had assisted him at the shop. He didn't give it much thought; he took off his glasses, pressed his eyes with his hands and took a deep sigh when he moved his hands away from his face. He took the box that his grandma gave him and put it in a drawer. He had an impulse, before putting the box away, to open and go through the pictures, however, he rushed to put it in the drawer and close it.

Then, he went to the kitchen to help his grandma prepare lunch. The time they spent together helped them both to forget about grandpa. Cooking was a pass-time that Ondřej enjoyed, especially when he had guests, so it distracted him enough. Shortly after, his mother called to let them know she had arrived at the train station with his siblings, if he would pick them up in his car.

The way to the train station was...strange. Again, in spite of having quite abstracted himself in the kitchen, the image of his grandfather came back to his mind like a stamp. He thought to have seen the face of his grandpa in various drivers, and also in some passersby. The weirdest was that it was not a unique face, he could notice the face of his grandpa at different ages. That brought his mind back to the image in the photograph and the young man at the shop in town: "Of course! It was the face of his young grandfather!" So, Ondřej had the ideas that his grandpa had had, maybe, some extramarital love affair, which he had managed to keep hidden until then. However, how was it possible that so many people had his traits? Could his grandpa have had more than one affair? Impossible! He couldn't have been involved with the whole town...the numbers didn't add up. Evidently, something was happening in his mind, in his head. His brain was not working well. There was something there that had collapsed, something lashed, that didn't move forward. He didn't quite understand why the memories of his grandpa were affecting him so much. Why? Why? WHY? He had always had trouble controlling his emotions; it was difficult for him, very difficult. However, this, in this way, had never happened to him before.

He was so affected by his grandfather's issue that, when he arrived at the station to pick up his mother and brothers, he begged it was them, he begged not to find in them faces other than the ones he was used to. Fortunately, they were themselves, so he sighed deeply in joy.

The fifteen minutes' drive that it took to get back to Svatá were quiet and he was distracted by the conversation with his family. However, once they went into town, his grandfather's face, scattered around in the faces of several people, appeared again and took him away from the conversation. He felt abstracted until his mother caught his attention by repeating the same question three times and shaking him a bit by the right shoulder. Ondřej shook his head and acted as if nothing had happened, he acted as normal as if he had been doing business at work.

He didn't want to let show the feeling of dementia he was starting to have, at least for the time being.

He didn't want to demonstrate any sign that could be interpreted as the beginning of schizophrenia; since, anyway, it wasn't absolutely clear that he suffered from that, and probably he just needed to have some rest, sleep better or take a walk through the woods in front of his house.

"That man looks a lot like grandpa!" one of his brothers pointed out of the window as they passed by and continued to point at the man while turning to the rear windshield. "Wow!" he exclaimed, straightening up.

Ondřej didn't say anything, but at least that was the first sign that the talks with grandma were affecting not only him. His brothers Dominik and Daniel had been with her the day before as well, there in Svatá, so it was not illogical to conclude that the lady had quite got into the head of the three.

"Hey, it's true!" "There's another!" pointed Daniel this time.

"I think that we have to get grandma to take it easy when talking about him," said Ondřej about the topic. "I have seen him around in several places today. It's affecting us."

"Stop speaking nonsense!" Daniela, their mother, interrupted. "Your grandma is old, let her express in any way she wants!"

"Mum, you're not with her all day." "I'm the one living with her," stated Ondřej. And he was right.

Ondřej slowed down, turned the steering wheel to the right and the tires rode on a dirt road. Some meters ahead, he turned right again, and in no time, they were back at the house. Grandma had already prepared lunch, the table was set, so they came in and ate.

After lunch, they prepared coffee and went out to have it in the garden. The weather was perfect for staying out. Clear sky. No wind. Temperature slightly over 15 degrees Celsius. It was nice. They sat around the table and the first topic to come out of the lady's mouth was *grandpa;* however, her grandchildren overtook her and lead the conversation in a different direction.

Shortly after, grandma got up saying she was going to look at something on the neighbor's flowers, which lied next to the wire fence. They noted something strange in her.

Before standing up, Dominik had pointed in her direction with his head to Ondřej so that he could keep an eye on her. They exchanged a quick raise of their eyebrows and a slight stretching of upper lips; they didn't say anything and went on with the conversation they were engaged in, even though they noticed her look fixed on some static point in the garden, as if lost.

Suddenly, they heard her shout and turned around, startled. She was astonished, looking into the neighbor's garden. From far, all four asked her, almost in unison, what had happened, but grandma didn't answer. After a few seconds, she turned around and went towards them quite more hurriedly than she usually walked. She moved her lips, as if mumbling something but emitted no words.

Halfway, she stopped, and hold on to a tall young pine tree in her garden. The grandchildren saw how her face transformed completely into something impossible to describe; it was not surprise, it was not anguish; it was not the look of nostalgia; however, it was all of that, absolutely all of those. She started crying, her body started crying out of the inability to express itself and not knowing what to express either. She was shocked.

Her daughter and grandchildren stood up immediately and approached her. Until she lifted her head to look at them in the eyes and pointed to the neighbor's house. Her shoulder was shaking so hard that her finger received an incomparable convulsion, so that they didn't actually know which way she was pointing. They knew it was the neighbor's house because of the direction of the arm, but her hand was shaking so hard up and down already that it would indicate any cardinal point.

"Grandpa...", she mumbled unexpectedly.

Everyone exchanged looks of confusion.

Then, her legs went weak and she asked for the assistance of her grandchildren to get seated on the ground. They tried to keep her upright, but she asked them to let her down, she needed to get in contact with the earth.

"You three, go and see," suggested the mother of the young men, worried enough to pay a visit to their neighbor and find out what had upset grandma so much, what was actually happening with grandpa. "I'll stay with grandma."

Ondřej, Daniel and Dominik went out on the street, went to the house next door and knocked. Ondřej took advantage of the short way to finally tell his brothers quickly what had happened in the morning without sounding crazy. Daniel and Dominik looked at him funny; they didn't consider him crazy but they looked at him in a funny way because, to a certain extent, they actually believed him; in spite of how unbelievable the story sounded, since they too thought to have seen their grandfather. Unless all of them were suffering from some strange obsessive memory disorder! Go figure which demential connections their neurons were making inside their brains, for God's sake!

They heard the bell ringing from outside and fifteen seconds later a man and a woman appeared at the door, greeting them with a grin in their faces. And the three brothers opened their eyes wide, and swallowed with some difficulty! The face of their grandfather was on both visitors, although the couple didn't seem to have realized. Even though it wasn't a hundred percent defined face, the traits were definitely those of their grandfather's, without the slightest doubt.

"Good morning, neighbors!" "How are you?", asked the woman.

None of the brothers replied.

"Is something the matter?" the man wondered, first looking at his wife, exchanging confused looks with her, since he didn't understand what was happening to the young men; and he turned his look towards Ondřej

." No, no." "Nothing's the matter," Ondřcj reacted quickly. Suddenly, he thought of asking: "It's just that my grandma was wondering if…if you had liked the walnuts!", he came up with this as he fleetingly remembered that they had bought some the day before.

"Wonderful!" the lady answered, lifting her hands up to her chest and softly shaking them.

"Yes, great" said the man, and showed them one he had in his hand. He put it in his mouth and. while chewing, he added: "Delicious!"

The three brothers smiled.

"Would you like some more?" it occurred to Daniel.

"No, thanks. We still have some" answered the woman

"Good. Well, just that…Have a nice afternoon!" closed Dominik. He waved goodbye, turned around and started walking back into the house. Daniel and Ondřej followed him.

The went across the iron gate and entered their garden. They saw their mother kneeling next to their grandma beside the pine tree, and they noticed that they seemed to be hypnotized, looking in the same direction.

Both their looks pointed in the direction of the walnut tree. There was no wind, but the branches have started to swing, as if they were wrapping themselves around an ethereal whirlwind. It was strange… Ondřej even got closer to take a look at the tree, because he believed to have detected something besides the movement of the branches up high.

He stood under the tree top and, approaching the trunk with his half-closed eyes in a scrutinizing look, he softly caressed it; and he immediately took his hand away, as he perceived how the wood seemed to withdraw lightly and subtly! As if one of the wrinkles if the trunk had moved with such a noble delicacy as would a disguised caterpillar.

Ondřej walked away from the walnut tree and turned to help take his grandmother inside. They tried to forget about their grandpa for a while, so they didn't bring up the subject again all day. In the evening, the young man took his mother and brothers to the train station. When he returned, he had dinner with his grandma while watching a film on television. Before going to bed, as usual, he went out to the porch for a smoke. He lit it and stood in his typical position: with the left arm crossed and his hand under his armpit. He smoked it completely without taking his look away from the walnut tree, noticing that it was still moving even though there was no wind.

"Ondro, Ondro!" his grandma cried from downstairs. "Ondro, Ondro!"

Ondřej, scared, took a leap and hit his head against the ceiling. He put his robe on and came down the stairs as fast as he could. His grandmother laid waiting at the foot of the stairs, her hands on the steps, her body leaning forward in the direction of her grandson's room in order to make her voice reach him more strongly.

"Ondro, Ondro!" she insisted over and over again.

"What's the matter? What's wrong?" he asked, desperately, holding her by the shoulders. "Calm down, calm down!" she insisted when she felt his nervousness through her hands. It was electrifying and chilling. He had to calm her down, otherwise she could suffer a heart attack or emotional shock again, as she had the day before, or worse.

The woman didn't say anything else and, with her arm shaking like a malnourished, naked boy standing outside in the winter, she pointed outward. Ondřej turned his head in the indicated direction and he did nothing else but opening his eyes wide. His eyelids exerted an incredibly extraordinary strength in order to contain his organs and for them not to jump like pirates off the plunge.

Their garden was so crowded with people that those who didn't fit there stood on the street. They were crammed as a compact butter cookie dough made by a boy while he's watching cartoons on TV and who licks the butter off his fingers every once in a while.

When Ondřej approached the door to see through the glass, he noted they were all contemplating the walnut tree, stupefied, as if the tree was some kind of god. There was no room left, not even for an ant to find a way through the grass. No. No space. Any ant would have suffocated to death. People were swinging ethereally, from side to side, as if possessed by a strange pharmacological vapor in a dance that seemed sedative, anxiolytic, muscle relaxant and hypnotic. At that moment, the lady got closer to his grandson to see what those people were doing in their garden.

Strangely -though it wasn't that weird anymore-, Ondřej managed to see his grandfather in different versions, at different ages. All of the people there were Miroslav: taller, shorter; at age fifteen; at his eighteen; in his twenties; at his twenty-five; in his thirties; in his forties, and so on…with hair, bald, well built, thinner, with breasts, without them…but all of the faces were his. There was no doubt: it was Miroslav.

Ondřej could make out his neighbors from the crowd; and he did it because they were wearing the same clothes as the previous day. He noted, then, the woman who had assisted him at the little shop and several other people who… *HAD BOUGHT WALNUTS THE OTHER DAY!*, he reacted suddenly.

Behind his grandfather's face's mask were all the people from the town who had bought and eaten the walnuts from the tree where his grandfather ashes had been planted, cultivates and buried. *The walnut tree had absorbed his ashes,* he gathered to himself, wishing to close the circle, *split between the trunk, branches and fruit...*He then followed the tree with his eyes, from the base to the cup, and... *PANEBOŽE!*, he expressed when he saw the cup of the tree, which left him jaw-dropped: all the branches and leaves made up the face of his grandfather.

Then, the fruit were distributed in town, he continued to think; *people ate them, and the body of my grandfather is...regenerating in them?*, he scanned once more the rest of the people who had gathered around his house. Now... why not them? *Why hadn't them* -his brothers, his mother, as well as their grandma or Ondřej himself, *suffered any transformation?* he reflected. *Maybe because we are blood relatives, because we are his heirs? Or because he didn't feel like "infecting" us? Or because we've had the nuts baked? Because he hates us? Because he loves us? Because he wants to come back to tell us that he didn't like where he was buried, and wants us to be buried somewhere else? Because he didn't want to be cremated?* "*PANEBOŽE!*" he exclaimed again. His head was about to explode.

Suddenly, people started moving; they started walking towards the walnut tree. Previously, the had stayed quite far from it, about three meters away, but now they were advancing towards it. Through the glass, he could see people disappearing as they approached the tree and he blinked several times, astonished, until he realized that people were really vanishing right before his eyes. He immediately opened the door and shouted, desperately, in the thought that one of the old drainage wells near the tree had collapsed and people were falling in there. However, when he came out to the porch, he put more attention, noticing that no one had turned to see that he was there. They were all hypnotized and lured by the walnut tree as if it was a magnet.

People disappeared upon crossing the radius that had previously kept them apart from the trunk; that is, when entering the six meters in diameter that surrounded the trunk of the tree.

Ondřej moved forward in the porch and stood in his toe tips to have better sight of what was happening near the tree, and he was stunned when he noticed that people were swallowed by the ground as if there was quicksand within that circle. Not only that, but as people were sucked in by the ground, it could also be seen how the bodies were transported along the trunk up to the tip of some branch of the walnut tree and then they disappeared. The skin of the tree looked as gelatinous and flexible as a pregnant woman's womb, and people could clearly be seen going through, just as a child moving in their mother's womb trying to find the right position to nap, and at the same speed as blood running through vessels.

Ondřej held his head with his hands. He didn't know how to react. Especially, when he realized that the walnut tree was acquiring the shape of his grandfather as it swallowed people, as if they were sweets.

He didn't know whether to call the police, or get among the crowd and try to slap them awake or shake them into consciousness; whether to go get the axe or gasoline to set the tree on fire... He looked in every direction, into every corner he could reach at that moment from where he was; however, he saw nothing.

Right then, his grandmother came into the porch and let Jerry out, who went directly to the middle of the crowd to greet people; however, no one paid attention to him, and he turned to Ondřej. Grandma had also approached him and held him by the arm with both hands, astonished at what she was seeing.

"What do we do?" she dares ask while she contemplated the situation in absolute horror.

"I don't know, grandma" "I don't know," he mumbled, awestruck at how the walnut tree was, little by little, acquiring his grandfather shape. "I thought we could burn it, but if I get close, the ground will swallow me as well. People don't react, either".

"An entire town vanished!" the lady expressed. "What will we tell the police?!"

Ondřej simply and with some difficulty at the same time, breathed deeply. He inhaled through his nostrils, held the air in his chest and cheeks for some seconds and, immediately after he let it out through the mouth, very slowly, emptying his cheeks last. He didn't say one word; he didn't have any.

"Is this murder, Ondro?" asked the old lady.

"I don't know, grandma," he scratched his head with his right hand while looking at how people kept moving forward, kept being absorbed by the ground, and then by the walnut tree roots.

"If I wanted to see grandpa again, would it be murder?" the woman reformulated her question.

"Do you want to see grandpa?" Ondřej looked at her with wide open eyes, surprised with what he was asking his grandma.

"I need to see him," she paused and focused her pupils on the walnut tree, which had already transmuted its aspect into her late husband's. She added: "And maybe he needs to see me, Ondro. He's doing all this for a reason."

They stood there, motionless, just watching until everything was over; until all the people disappeared from the garden and the tree had completely turned into Miroslav. The walnut tree shrunk until it acquired the built that the man had had before dying: the few leaves that were left secluded themselves in the branches and, at the same time, the branches were absorbed by the trunk; this, in turn, compressed itself down to one meter and sixty-something centromeres of height while the branches which had been absorbed formed the wrinkles, cuts, traits and expressions in the face, neck, torso and limbs. Finally, the eyelashes slowly opened and his clear eyes showed, accompanied by a smile.

Ondřej and his grandmother were stunned, more than ever in their lives, when they glimpsed at the sparkle in his eyes and notices it was identical to the one he showed when he was alive, the same as the serenity that embraced him at all levels.

"Miroslav?" whispered the lady softly, astounded, as if showered by a glacial water bucket, from the porch. So softly that she didn't even know if her grandson, who was right by her side, had heard her. However, she saw her husband nodding and smiling even more. Then, her heart started beating faster and pumping more strongly, so that nothing but what she was feeling at that moment was necessary as an answer.

The woman noticed that her husband couldn't move from where he was standing, he was still rooted there. The roots had not turned into feet, so he couldn't lift them, the roots were too heavy. Then, she suddenly reacted: she let go off her grandson and ran towards her husband.

There was no pain in her knee that would prevent her from doing that. At least, she didn't feel any pain. Her adrenal gland had taken charge of providing with and immediate and superlative shot of adrenaline to add to the quantity already in her circulating blood in order for her to overcome this emotion. Even her grandson, taking her quickly by the arm, however she loosened and continued her sprint towards her love.

Since he couldn't stop her, Ondřej followed her but he couldn't even catch her shadow as grandma was moving very fast. He shouted at her, but it didn't work either. There was no way of stopping her, no point in obstructing her path. And he was afraid for her...he didn't want her too to be swallowed by the ground.

The lady stopped right in front of the shape of the walnut tree, nose to nose. Ondřej choked a cry of horror when grandma went over the limit of that imaginary circle inside of which people were gulped by the roots of the tree as you do a cold beer in the summer. Nevertheless, and luckily, none of that happened; and so, his soul went back into Ondřej's body, so he took his hand to his chest.

"Miroslav!" she expressed with tears in her eyes and a smile that appeared and disappeared spasmodically, as if she was suffering from a happiness hiccup.

"Zdeňka!"

Without moving her eyes away from his, the woman slowly lifted her hands and touched his husband's arms from the tip of the fingers to the shoulders. She went with her hands over his neck and softly went up to his cheeks. She noticed he was still made of wood. Then she inhaled and noticed he smelled of wood also. But she didn't care. She explored his forehead with her fingers, from the sides, she bordered the edges of his eyebrows, just on top of them; when she reached the frown, she went up a few centimeters and then came back to the sides following the contour of the hairline.

After that, she came down with her thumbs gently along the lines of his jaws until they came together at the tip of the chin. She continued over the ears, from the lobes upwards; through the back and coming back to the lobes following the reverse path. Shortly, she went through the neck up to the back of the head, and went by the occipital bone to the top; and then came back down...to the jaws; where she placed her pinkies, and the rest of the fingers, as if playing an ethereal song on a fragile string harp, laid on his cheeks again.

"It's you" she exclaimed with a whisper that only he could hear.

He nodded. Ondřej got as close as he could, slowly. Jerry stood by his side; strangely, he hadn't run to his grandfather as he would with any other visitor.

"Why are you here?" she wanted to know. The smile on his face that was coming and going, finally stayed in his face, extended from ear to ear.

"Do you remember what day is today?" He asked her, spreading his arms and taking her softly by the waist, as when they were teenagers.

She nodded in denial.

"The day we planted this tree as a symbol of our love and I promised I would never be away from you. Here. Exactly as we are right now: you holding me by the face and I holding you by the waist. Looking at your eyes though seeing your soul."

The woman stood in silence for a few seconds, during which she bit her lips and let out a couple of tears that she didn't wish to dry. These rolled down her cheeks as riderless horses in a prairie, happy, with an endless joy, playing as young foals breaking into adolescence and playing foolishly.

"Here is where it all started, *Zdeňko*" continued the man. "Here. And I know you haven't forgotten! You may have forgotten that day, but not the essence of this walnut tree. There's a reason why this tree is important to me. There's a reason why this tree is important to you.

A few other tears that had gathered in her eyes overflowed the lower eyelid, as a bathtub left with the tap open.

"Will you stay?" the woman wanted to inquire.

"Yes."

"Like this? Forever?"

Ondřej opened his eyes wide: a whole town couldn't disappear because of his grandfather!

"No, sweetheart" answered Miroslav, while he wiped one of her tears.

At that moment, Ondřej left out a sigh of relief. Even though he didn't know for sure what would happen to the town people yet.

"Each one of us," the man continued to explain, wiping his wife's other cheek with the thumb, "belongs to a different cosmos."

The woman observed without understanding it all.

The man put his right index finger on her left breast. The woman felt something strange in her heart at that moment, a prick, a sting right to the center of her pumping organ. The man inhaled deeply. He held the air for a few seconds in his chest. He left it out in a rested uniform way. And keeping his finger in place still, he said:

"Here," he paused again, though for a shorter time, and added: "Forever. As a memory, beating, beating in the ones that are alive." Then, he extended his arms to the sky and shook his head, expressing with joy: "As a walnut tree! The interlace of life and death" and immediately upon his saying this, his body took the shape of a walnut tree in the blink of an eye, and there was small swirl that made the woman's hair fly a bit, as well as their grandson's, who was a couple of steps away. Jerry, on the other hand, dashed in fear, and hid under the porch table.

"D*obrý den, Zdeňko!"* she was greeted.

The young man and the lady turned upon hearing the voice. Form the other side of the fence, their neighbor- just as usual, with her usual face; and her husband appeared right away to say hello. Even he was *himself*.

Zdeňka as well as Ondřej, somewhat stunned, returned the greeting and then looked at each other. Then, she observed the tree, from the trunk to the leaves. Ondřej got closer to her and held her by the shoulders, and he insisted on going inside. She accepted.

Once inside, the young man sat in the armchair that his grandpa used to sit in, and his grandma sat at the foot of the bed opposite the chair, on the other side of the coffee table, and in front of the television set. A cup of coffee in her hands, her torso leaning forward and her elbows on the seams of her skirt, her look went through the glass door and fixed on the walnut tree.

Ondřej contemplated his grandmother with care and curiosity; he straightened up a little in his seat, and turned his head to look at the tree, thinking that something was happening around it once again, but no, nothing was going on. It was still. He looked back at his grandma and leaned back on the armchair. He sipped a bit of coffee.

"Grandma, are you okay?"

"Yes, yes…" she responded quickly. "It's just that..." she took her hand to her chest, as wanting to grab her heart, she felt a sharp pain right in the center, as if something was growing roots in there. She immediately shook her head, and took her hand off her chest to hold the cup, and stared at her grandson: "What do you think that grandpa came to see me for?"

"I don't know…What has he told you? I haven't heard much, you were whispering. I only heard what he said before he turned back into a tree."

"And what do you think it means?"

Ondřej shrugged his shoulders, not knowing what to answer…and he sipped his coffee.

That was clearly not the best day for Ondřej. As a family, they had decided, the same as with grandpa some years before, to cremate the body and preserve it in a different state, and his mother had just called him to ask him to go with her get the remains. So, after he finished working, he got into his car and pick up his mother to go to the crematorium.

They parked at the front, got off the car and rang the bell of the front door. A bald man answered and let them in. The man offered them a seat in front of a desk and asked them for some information. The young man noticed his mother was nervous because she couldn't stop stumping her foot on the floor, so he reached out for her hand, which was lying on her knee. And the frantic movement of her leg stopped immediately.

Then, the bald man stood up and disappeared behind a door. A few minutes later, he returned with a special ceramic vase - previously chosen by Ondřej's mother- and placed on top of the desk. Ondřej saw his mother swallow with some difficulty, suppressing a deep sadness and her tears. He approached her and asked her if she'd rather wait in the hallway; she nodded in acceptance, without uttering a word, stood up and left the room.

"Mr. Kočovsky", said the man when he saw the woman had closed the door. "Here is your grandmother," the man indicated gently pushing the vase in his direction, but never taking his hands off it. He looked him right in the eye, and added: "But there is something you need to know…"

Ondřej looked at him in surprise.

The man put his hands on top of the lid.

"There is something that were not able to cremate", he said with his eyes wide open. He then took the lid off the vase and immediately leaned it forward to show him the contents.

Ondřej was shocked: on top of the ashes lied a walnut.

He lifted his look up to the man and back to the nut. He put his hand inside the jar, took the nut and put it in front if his eyes. Some seconds later, he jumped from his chair and gave a cry of fright, as if he had been electrocuted. He dropped the nut and it fell on the floor. He observed it from above...

"What's the matter?" asked the bald man with curiosity.

"Nothing..." lied Ondřej, without taking his eyes away from the nut, which was now at his feet. A chill had wrapped him up, from head to toes in a second, after having felt on his fingers a rhythmic beating that came from inside the nutshell...a pumping. A heartbeat...

"Are you sure, Mr. Kočovsky?!"

"Yes, yes...erm...nothing's the matter," he repeated quickly and immediately bent, took the nut and put it in his pocket. He then approached the desk, put the lid on the vase while he thanked the bald man, and took the nut with him. He said goodbye upon leaving.

On the way home, he took his mother to her apartment. He didn't tell her anything about the walnut, even though he could feel it beating in against his thigh in his pocket and every beat was appalling. When they arrived, he handed the vase with the remains of his grandma over to his mother and walked her up to her apartment door on the fourth floor. Daniela told her son she was feeling better when her son asked again if she needed anything else, so they greeted goodbye and he drove fifty kilometers back to his house in the town of Svatá, on the number 191. It wasn't easy for him to drive with the nut beating against his leg, so he took it out of his pocket and put it on the passenger's seat. However, it wasn't easy either to drive with the nut there: he could perceive the pulses in his brain and his look turned nervously to it every once in a while.

When he arrived, fortunately safe and sound, he took the nut from the seat and walked with it up to the walnut tree. He walked towards the tree as if he was going to confront his grandfather and then he stopped bluntly, halfway between the car parked by the side of the house and the tree...

He looked at the walnut in his trembling hands.

He looked at the walnut tree.

He breathed.

Looked at the nut. Felt its beating.

Looked at the tree.

Breathed.

He looked at the nut again and noticed that his hands weren't trembling anymore. He wasn't scared.

He looked at the walnut tree.

And smiled.

He was happy.

Looked at the nut. Felt its beating. Smiled. Laughed. He rejoiced.

And he heard his grandma asking to his ear once more, after so many years: *"And what do you think it means?"*

After so many years, Ondřej finally understood the real meaning of what his grandpa had once come to tell his grandma: the interweaving of life and death.

It only remained one decision to make: to bury it or to keep her. Either way, her memory would beat forever.

A kiss on the forehead

*To my grandfather and
my mother. Especially her,
who knows well...*

Many say that things should be called by their names to face and overcome them. On the other hand, there is one in particular that becomes more powerful and resistant just by naming it. The only way to defeat her is to attack her as she attacks.

Antonio lived in a nursing home where he was cared for very well; he was also fortunate that his middle daughter, Claudia, visited him almost every day., unless she had to babysit her grandson, who was in that moment six months old. From time to time she would go with him during visiting hours and show him to her father. She would sit himon his lap and Antonio would try to play by moving his hands very slowly; and the most beautiful thing of all was that this made him smile.

Antonio was an Italian immigrant with robust hands, a typical fine anchovy mustache, and a righteous soul. He had migrated to Buenos Aires at the age of 14 around 1940 and was getting close to turning 90. However, he had not been the same Antonio for a couple of years. Apart from old age, a very strong hurricane wind had risen through the corridors of that great library called memory which is well sunk in the mysterious and magical brain nebula, sweeping away a large number of pieces... books, photos, paintings, landscapes, papers, the very same shelves... leaving empty puzzles, which told stories once the missing piece was found. And,as time went by, more powerful and sinister winds came and extinguished the chandeliers that illuminated those corridors, leaving them dark and inhospitable, and they took more and more pieces of the puzzles making Antonio more of a shell than Antonio himself, making of him more like a tortoise shell but without its inhabitant in it.

To wake up every day was to find oneself in an uncertain and different point in the middle of the eternal and dark night of those corridors. Walking through and between them was... it was... indescribably sad, at all; it was to find -perhaps, perhaps! - some of those pieces of a puzzle related to some part of his memory and to try to find out where that piece of sky, or cloud, or ground, or hand or eye belonged to.

However, there was a kind of Noah's Ark, in which he could shelter from the storms that made his mind a tidal wave of chills; there was the place where he took the pieces that he found, to that ship located in who-knows-what horizon in the confines of his most primitive memory, rooted in the basement of that enormous library with as many floors as Antonio was years old. However, it was not easy to find it, since he did not know on which floor or in which hallway he woke up. He could probably have some notion according to the degree of clarity of that one: the denser and blacker the reigning gloom, the higher it was located in the building. Manifestly, that which had seized him, had thrown itself like a curtain overhead, embracing everything and sliding slowly and in a macabre way through the windows like concentrated paint, caked, like burning tar... although what at first was slow, it became accelerated in a blink, vertiginous, and there were almost no windows left to cover, except for the occasional space where a timid beam of light managed to filter fearfully.

The question, basically, was to locate the staircase that communicated with the floor below, and so on at each floor; but it was not easy, since the stairs were not connected to each other: each floor had to be swept to come across the corresponding staircase that would take to the underlying one. It happened sometimes -to tell the truth, *almost always*, and as time went on and on, the word *always* gained more strength and notoriety, becoming capitalized letter by letter, maturing in its meaning while putting the word *almost* aside- that he slept hugging the piece of a puzzle, and the next day he woke up without it, being that some diabolical shadow had stolen it while he was asleep.

In such an unshakable ship -although with some cracks already in parts from the fateful blows of dark waves and the very attack of sinister and blackened apocalyptic creatures. These creatures had tried to darken Antonio's entire interior and lashed inside his head every day with more strength, making the fight more and more difficult- Antonio kept his most powerful memories and collected the pieces of puzzles that he managed to carry each day with greater difficulty, though always fighting.

Antonio knew clearly that one day he would have to set sail on his ship and leave many pieces of his memory lost there in the library of his mind. Still, it was the best he could do. That skyscraper was packed and riddled with gloom and it wouldn't be long before ALL the shadows finally found the ship and destroyed it with everything he had collected, and more! It would not be fair... and it would be excruciatingly painful, since such emotion would squeeze his heart to the point where it would stop him at the slightest sigh of sorrow.

A couple of days passed until Claudia agreed to go visit her father with her grandson. She had already gone, however, without him. Antonio noticed that she had come when his great-grandson's feet touched his lap: inside him, everything became clearer; sadly, not much, though it was a nice miracle that it happened at least to such an extent ... Every time the child appeared and touched him, a magical light managed to filter -who knows how- through some of the windows, regardless of whether they were completely hidden under the blackness, and certain corridors got some light that made his memories on the shelves become novel. Many times, he used that light that came off that child to take a book and read it again... to relive... and laugh... and smile... and be happy...

He felt immediately as if a fire alarm was going off until his ears were stunned: he had to flee NOW! He had to take advantage of the light to find the stairs, go down the necessary number of floors to the ship, and raise anchor! He didn't know how many more of these opportunities he would have left, and he thought that what he had already carried was enough.

He descended each staircase at a speed he could never have imagined, and despite the restlessness, he did not hesitate for a second to stop. He didn't really know what floor he was on; he didn't want to find out either. He just had to get down, get down and keep going down until he came across the ship before the light disappeared. And then, when the time came, he would set sail.

"Well… it's time to go…" he heard Claudia say in such a friendly and childish way, which led him to think she was addressing the baby.

DO NOT! Antonio exclaimed; he had not yet reached the boat. It was just a few steps away. Such an opportunity could not be missed. He could see behind him how the night was falling again. Flagrantly, there was more clearness around the ark than in other parts of the building, but -come on! -it didn't make much difference anyways.

"Let's say *goodbye* to grandpa ..." Claudia added after taking her grandson under the armpits and pulling him away from the old man's thighs.

Almost, almost now!, jumped into the Ark of Memories.

"Bye *grandpa...*" Claudia spoke as if she was her own grandson. She rested the boy's forehead on the old man's lips and he pursed his lips.

YES!, sighed Antonio happily. He had weighed anchor.

Laureano had seen his grandmother sitting alone, drinking mate under the shade of some branches of an ombú tree that had been reborn after being cut down for ruining the floor of the house ten years before. The little boy came over and sat next to her. Claudia poured him a mate and handed it to him with a smile.

"What are you thinking, Grandma?" he asked curiously, noticing her thoughtfully, with her gaze inward.

"Today would be your grandpa's birthday.

"Antonio?" he asked and sucked on the metal straw.

She nodded and pressed her lips. She looked at the horizon at that moment. She sighed deeply and after releasing the air, added to the gesture of assent:

"Yeah, him..." Then she looked at her grandson and she handed him the mate back. She admired how big he was, how much he had grown. While she was brewing a mate for her, she dared to ask: "Do you remember him?

"He's the one in the photos, right?

"Yes." He drank from the straw.

"No. Well, something," he corrected himself quickly, since he felt that he might hurt his grandmother and he didn't feel like doing it. He preferred to lie at that moment and then he would see what he could make up; he would at least try, try to remember something, and if it wasn'ttrue, his grandmother would correct him.

"What do you remember? Because you were a baby…" the mate finished. He tipped the kettle, put more water in it, and handed it to his grandson.

Laureano grabbed the mate while thinking… thinking…

"I remember he kissed me on the forehead.

"I always made him give you kisses on the forehead.

"Yes ..." he sucked on the straw, "but I remember one in particular."

Claudia looked at him strangely. She frowned.

"In fact…" He felt that a lamp had lit inside him. "I can tell you many things about your dad!" He added enthusiastically.

His grandmother took the mate and challenged him:

"Let's see! What do you have to tell me?!

Laureano finished the mate and reached over his hand to give the mate to his grandmother. She extended hers and caught it, however the young boy did not let the mate go. At that moment, he brought his other hand to the mate and placed it on top of his grandmother'shand, caressing it delicately, to which he whispered *Do you want to see me?* Immediately and for an instant, Claudia felt as if she had put her fingers into the socket; immaculate and powerful electricity invaded her body, kicking her in the spinal cord and shaking it all. Endless emotions were knotted in her throat and they did not know how to express themselves, how to untie themselves, how to continue before what came later on...

Suddenly, Claudia found herself in the middle of a huge library. A hand stroked her back and she jumped.

"Come," his grandson said in a low voice, almost as a weak breath, and they held hands… slowly but firmly.

At that moment, the woman felt that it was not her grandson who was holding her hand. He had incredible strength, just as her father would have grabbed her when she was little to cross the street.

Laureano led his grandmother down a corridor to a staircase at the end. They descended one floor, walked through the corridors of another set of shelves full of books and things until they reached a new staircase that continued down. They went down again. And so, they continued for ten floors, between corridors, stairs and shelves ... During the trip, there was no space to say anything to each other. The perplexity that Claudia carried with her had not allowed it; Laureano, on the other hand, had chosen to remain silent and only look at his grandmother from time to time and smile at her.

When they reached the underground, the atmosphere was completely different. As he opened the door to the staircase that would take them there, a sea-scented air rose in her nostrils. After the last step, white sand spread out into a calm sea of low, serene waves. To one side, there was a ship, somewhat undone, rarely docked in the sand, as if it had been spat out by a sea attacked by a raging flu.

Laureano accompanied his grandmother to that ship, right up to an opening in its side. There, he ushered her in first and, without letting go of her hand, led her inside... Claudia contemplated amazed at what she was seeing. It didn't look like the inside of a ship at all. Its interior design, though it was not accurate, appeared to be an unfinished puzzle, made her feel inside her house of Longchamps where she had lived, there on Langhenein street. The woman was also surrounded by fabulous things: there were photos, many of them from the old days, of her, of her brothers Marcelo and Walter, of her children, of her mother Amelia, that photo of the wedding where Antonio had had to step up -discreetly! - one step higher on the stairs than his wife so as not to appear shorter... There was a small-scale replica of his old Citröen 2CV on a piece of furniture that her father had driven until his health no longer allowed him; there were books with worn pages, with faded phrases; on the spines, these books read titles such as: *"Working at Siemens", "Anecdotes of the year 90", " Amelia, love of my life", "My mother, Nonna" or "Claudia"* ...

After looking around, she looked at herself and realized she had mutated into a 16-year-old girl. She had discovered herself physically identical to her daughter Daniela, Laureano's mother, when she saw herself in the reflection of the glass of one of the photos. Then she turned around and saw that her grandson's hand had also changed, was larger and filled with wrinkles. Then, Laureano entered and his body immediately grew taller and larger as he crossed the threshold of that hollow in the ship.

The knot that had begun to strangle Claudia´s throat just immediately after her skin was found itself in the house of Langhenein, was caked in her trachea that her eyes began to fill with tears. And in the middle of the silence, she launched herself to hug the man in front of her.

The hug seemed eternal. When they broke loose and he looked into her eyes, he said:

"Love you. Thanks". He reached into his pocket, handed her something, and closed her hand gently. "I will always be in the memory of your grandson.

"I love you ..."she stammered ... was the only thing she could say.

"We have won this battle together.

"I love you ..."she repeated. Her cheeks were wet in tears.

"Nothing has been able to erase my memory, and it is thanks to you.

"I love you ..."She could not utter anything else.

"Nothing could erase you.

"Love you…

"I love you too daughter.

Then Claudia blinked and found herself back under the ombú, drinking mate with her grandson. There was no boat, no beach, nor her house in Langhenein... nor her father... Between her and Laureano, they still held the mate, although the woman, unlike Laureano, lay with her face soaked and her eyes swollen with tears silent of love. Faced with such a situation, she was startled, giving a hiccup.

Laureano smiled at her from across the table and straightened up, dropping the mate. Claudia grabbed it, holding it to her chest and looking, scared and confused, at the countryside around her. She realized then that something was bothering her between her hand and the mate she was holding. It was a kind of thick paper folded twice in half. She left the mate on the table and unfolded it...

In front of her eyes, she had discovered a photo. It was hers together with 6-months-old Laureano; she was picking him up and leading him to kiss her father's forehead. The last capture that Antonio had been able to make of his memory.

Omelette

•

*Sometimes things... happen
because they just do.*

It had been a long time since *Aunt Flo* had come to visit his wife, so Oswald stopped at the pharmacy to buy one of those gadgets that would let him know if Lily was pregnant or not. On the way home, with his elbow out of the window and driving comfortably with his right hand on the wheel through a deserted road, he would occasionally look at the *Evatest* in the plastic bag and *wonder* why it bore that name. He madly pondered unexplored paths of the etymology of the word; he wandered ignorantly through a maze of inexplicable ecclesiastical, biblical and apocalyptic reasons and laughed at his own claims in which he came to conclude.

He parked the F100 at his front door and went inside. Lily was preparing lunch; she had sent her husband to buy a couple of things that she lacked to finish it. Absolutely everything he had to buy would have fit into a bag, so he had to look twice to really check if he was carrying two of them and not one. Noticing that he was carrying a small bag in his left hand, she gave him a frowning look with a strange and curious air and asked:

"What is that, Os?"

He raised his eyebrows and couldn't hold back the excitement; he immediately smiled and flushed. He gave her a rather fluffy kiss, wrapped his other arm around her waist, and hugged her lovingly. Lily felt a whole electric current, still somewhat doubtful and curious yet joyful, flooding her from head to toe.

After kissing her, without releasing her hug, he stepped away a few inches and lifted the bag over his shoulder, showing it to her. Lily's eyes filled with tears and Oswald's accompanied the sentiment. The woman covered her mouth when she did not know what to say, she did not know how to respond to such infinite and new rush of happiness when she saw what was timidly hiding in the pharmacy bag. They both knew that they still had to find out the result of that test, but such an overwhelming feeling of joy had erupted because they felt *TODAY was* the day that they *would* confirm *IT*, they felt *THEY WERE PREGNANT*.

Lily took the bag and ran to the bathroom. Oswald followed hot on her heels.

"Love, you're going to fall! Careful with the tummy!" He warned her as if the test had already given them a positive result.

Lily went into the bathroom and slammed the door in her husband's face.

"What are you doing? I want to see the result…"

"I'll tell you later." She bolted the door. She didn't want anything, not even the tiniest fly to bother her. "I must be calm, Oswald."

Oswald was on the other side of the door, with his ear resting on it. He could feel the noise of the bag and the paper wrapbreaking like a Christmas present for a child and it tickled his stomach.

"How many lines?!"

"I just took it out of the box, Oswald!"

"Do you want me to help you?" He peeked through the keyhole, but saw nothing.

"I'm reading the instructions."

"It is easy. You have to…"

"Shut up, Oswald!" she interrupted him. "Leave me alone, I told you! Go away!"

What a mood! he thought and walked away from the door. Head down, like a tethered dog, he lumbered to the dining room table and sat there waiting.

Who knows how long Oswald spent looking at the walls, the floor, the corners and the ornaments that were hanging on the wall until he could not stand it anymore. There, sat on the chair, reduced to an inanimate object such as those ornaments, to a kind of statue perhaps, he felt it was time to stand up.

"Stay away, Oswald!" Lily yelled from the bathroom, her teeth clenched, grumbling like a pig defending its food. It was as if she had heard the chair squeak.

The man walked around the table a couple of times while gently stroking it with the tips of his right index and middle fingers. He was sighing deeply... He stopped in front of the shelf with books and read each of the titles on the spines; there weren't many, in fact. He kept walking and gazed through the window at the back of the house: it was big, very green, and empty. He imagined his future son *or daughter ... if it is a girl, I would like to name her Susan* - he mused with a smile- playing football, rugby, basketball, hide and seek, or simply running with their superheroes or dolls on the hands making them fly... He imagined a swing, a sandbox, a tree house, a...

"OSWAAAAAAAAAAAALD!!!"

Lily's scream startled him, and completely threw him off! He didn't get it, honestly. It had a certain joyful atmosphere, so it could clearly indicate that the test had come back positive. However, it also brought a bit of disappointment, which made the test clearly negative. But there was something else that made Lily's scream weird: ASTONISHMENT and TERROR. And it was what left Oswald stunned and paralyzed on the spot.

"OSWAAAAAAAAAAAALD!!!" Lily screamed again.

The man reacted and ran to the bathroom. He tried to open the door however it was still locked from the inside.

"Lily!" He looked for her through the keyhole.

"Oswald!" She approached the door. But she did not open it.

"Tell me Lily! What happened?!"

"I do not know!" She leaned against the door with her shoulder and dropped her temple to it as well.

"How come *I do not know*?! Open up!"

"I don't know if I'm pregnant", she replied, disregarding her husband's request to open the door for her.

"How many lines appeared?"

"None."

"What do you mean by *none*?!"

"DON'T YOU LISTEN TO ME?! NO STRIPES!" She kicked the door.

"Don't be mad, will you?"

"Are you deaf or are you playing Mr. Bean?!"
"Lily, Mr. Bean was mute, not deaf."
"Anyway, he was an idiot!"
"Calm down, please, Lily. You will hurt our baby."

Lily took a deep breath through her nose and exhaled through her mouth. She tried to calm down; her husband was right; this could upset the baby. Anyway, Oswald was on the other side of the door and didn't really know what had happened with the test. So she took another deep breath two or three more times.

"A line, at the very least, had to have come out" Oswald insisted after a moment of silence and also breathing heavily when he noticed that Lily had already relaxed a bit.

"That what came out was not a line, Oswald!"
"What came out then?"
"A circle."
"A circle?!" He was surprised.
"Yeah, well... it's not exactly a circle."
"Lily, what are you talking about?"

There was the sound of the latch. The woman had unlocked the door. She opened it and extended her arms to her husband, handing him something that she had hidden in her hands.

"It has an oval shape..." she said shrugging her shoulders and blushing, and spread her fingers, showing him what her palms where nesting.

"What's that, Lily?"
"An egg... I think so..."
"Did you lay an egg?!"

Lily nodded her head doubtfully and said again:

"I think so... yes."

Oswald took the egg carefully and looked at it against a backlight under the ceiling fan.

"Why didn't you tell me you were a mutant?" He turned to his wife.

Lily made a grimace with her face; her entire face wrinkled in who-knows how many question marks.

"I'll take you to Professor X" He grabbed her by the wrist.

"Don't be an ass, Oswald" She shook her arm and let go. "And give me my son!" She snatched the egg from him with her other hand.

"We have to go to the doctor, Lily."

"I'm not going anywhere" she snorted.

"We must know why you laid an egg, my love", he insisted, shrugging and looking into her eyes.

"I will not allow any kind of studies. Not me, not my son" She pressed the egg against her chest.

"That's an egg, Lily."

"Don't talk to Omelette like that!"

"Ome…who?" Oswald shook his head as if he was surrounded by a cloud of mosquitoes; he did not understand if what he had heard was true or if he was really living in a dream, so he not only shook his head but gently slapped himself twice in the face,

"… WHAT ?!"

"Omelette!"

"Did you named the egg Omelette?!"

"It's not an egg, Oswald!" She sentenced with a frown. However, her mood quickly changed and, with a smile and rocking the egg in her arms, she said, "He's our son! Don't you like his name?" She asked tenderly while scratching the shell with her index finger as if it was her belly.

Oswald did not know what to answer. He didn't know if his wife had completely lost it or if she was playing a prank on him. Lily did use to make that kind of jokes, but all this seemed to come seriously because of the genuineness of her gestures, though mostly because of the way she looked and rocked that egg. Then he thought of playing along as far as his patience could go… or his impatience!

"It's a generic name", Lily explained. "It can be male or female. Like *Ariel* or *Andrea*. Don't you like it?" She insisted watching him from the corner of her eye in that crouched position.

"Yes, yes. I like it, I like it." Oswald answered quickly scratching his head.

"Besides, it is a French name…" Lily went on.

Oswald faked a smile and nodded, playing along as he said he would do, though it was also difficult for him to play it cool.

"Like Hamlet," Lily continued.

"Hamlet was a prince of Denmark, not of France, Lily", he EXHALED losing that little desire 'to pretend' he had just acquired. Clearly Lily was upset.

"It doesn't matter! It's the essence what really matters, Oswald, it's a CLASSY name. Listen! *Prince* or *Princess Omelette*". She waved her hand as if the name entirely occupied the huge marquee of a theater.

"Isn't it cute?" She waited for her husband's approval.

"Lily ..." he huffed, dropped the weight of his body on one of his legs leaning, and scratched his head again, "why don't you make me an omelette with that egg, will you, and stop pestering me about this?"

The woman's face changed completely. Her pupils aimed directly at her husband and penetrated his brain like an electric butcher's saw to bone. She pierced them like a hole in the wall and made Oswald feel the blazing fire of Hell hotter than he could have ever imagined. Lily had transmuted into someone much worse than Lucifer. The apocalyptic claims that Oswald had originally considered about the etymology of the word *Evatest* were just planet Earth in the great dark universe: absolutely NOTHING. Lily was the real apocalypse. That look made a terribly cold feeling run through Oswald, paralyzing him where he was. Terror itself was in front of his eyes; It was difficult for him to even swallow saliva.

"I'm just going to tell you one thing, OSWALD", Lily warned him, pointing her finger at him in the middle of his brow.

Oswald believed that the tip of that index finger pointing to his forehead would fire a bullet and pierce his skull at any moment. He was clearly intimidated. He stopped and listened. *Yes, my queen*, he thought to himself.

"Anytime you touch our son..." Her voice was soft but threatening. She made a pause.

Oswald already knew what was coming after the break: after such calm ...

"I CUT YOUR EGGS" she howled and pointed fervently to his crotch "THOSE YOU HAVE HANGING UNUSED BETWEEN YOUR USELESS PENIS AND I'LL MAKE YOU THE OMELETTE" she pointed towards his chest "THAT YOU WANT TO EAT SO MUCH, OSWALD!" She tapped her index finger against her husband's chest.

Oswald's eyes widened like two fried eggs and he choked on the saliva that had accumulated behind his tongue.

Lily took a deep breath closing her eyes and regained her composure immediately. She added delicately but cynically:

"It is understandable that you do not know anything about cooking, if you never do it, my love: the omelette is made at least with TWO -she showed it with her fingers-eggs"with her gaze she pointed back quickly and again at the crotch. She immediately looked back to her husband's eyes. "I'll brood Omelette until it's born".

"Will you brood? WHAT?!" exclaimed Oswald. He did not want to say those words beyond his mouth. It was a thought, but it escaped from him.

"Are you not listening, Mr. Magoo?"

"Mr. Magoo was myopic, Lily, not deaf.

"It doesn't matter, he screwed up like you screw up! Don't you understand that the essence is what counts here? Step aside and let me through!" She told him and pushed him through, putting him to the side. "I must finish lunch."

Oswald had set the table as usual: he had placed his plate and Lily's facing each other so that they could look at each other and have a pleasant conversation; the two glasses, both napkins and silverware as well. She made grapefruit juice in a glass pitcher and set it aside as well. When Lily finished the salad -it had lettuce, tomato, onion, boiled potato and corn- Oswald brought the salad bowl to the table and she did so with the MEDIUM RARE steaks on a plate behind her husband. Oswald sat down. She did not. She went back to the kitchen to look for... *Omelette*, Oswald sighed -although he tried to hide it- when he saw how his wife brought the egg like a duke in an extravagant and elegant chair. The egg was in an old, circular porcelain basket that Lily had inherited from her grandmother, nestled in sawdust. However, that was not all. The girl had dressed him in a black and white checkered harlequin hat from one of those childhood dolls that she kept in a box. She placed the basket on the side of the table.

Oswald rose up from his chair and took Lily's plate to serve. He used not to forget modesty and courtesy above all things, great bases of his education; since Lily was the cook, he responded with another gesture of gratitude, kindness, and condescension to his wife. However, as soon as he pricked a steak with his fork, Lily stopped him immediately:

"I'll eat salad, my love," she said and quickly turned to the egg and gently lost herself scratching the shell.

"But you like meat..." he pointed out stammering while looking at his wife scratching the egg.

Lily just glanced at him sharply and it was only enough for her husband to say nothing. Oswald served himself the piece of meat and then took the salad bowl and served his wife the vegetables. Then he served himself.

"Love..." said her husband, sitting down and taking both cutleries to start eating.

Lily sat up in her seat with a last smile that she directed at her son and took the fork. Pricking a piece of tomato, she replied:

"Tell me…

"I've been thinking... If you really want to raise that egg..." Oswald suddenly realized that he had just screwed up, that he had to measure his words when talking about the egg, since Lily's face twisted in a blink like Dr. Jekyll into Mr. Hyde.

Lily's sensitivity reached such a limit that Oswald had to watch every word because he would wake up with a knife through his leg, arm, or penis any moment. Lily didn't murder, not even a fly. She was capable of catching it with some bait and, once she had it between her claws, like cat to mouse, she would cut off a wing. Lily was only looking for the other's pain; she said that if her victim died, he would no longer suffer: once dead, he no longer suffers, and Lily did not enjoy either! She rejoiced in that cruel game. And although it was difficult to make his wife reach such an extreme point of revenge, with this egg... mmm... everything had disrupted a bit and probably her neurons were not helping in the necessary synapse that kept Lily's sanity.

"Yes, REALLY," said Lily interrupting him and killing him with her look, "I want to raise OUR SON," she corrected him again with intensity, "Oswald."

An awkward silence immediately filled the room, where the man preferred not to continue with what he was saying. He did not wish to sink deeper and deeper into that clearly swampy land which certainly belonged to his wife; Therefore, he stayed more than necessary chewing the piece of meat that he had brought to his mouth. However, she took it upon herself to make him swallow it forcing him to continue:

"What have you thought of? What were you going to tell me, Oswald?

Oswald forced the chunk of meat through his esophagus with a blow to his chest.

"I was saying that...

"Tell me ..." She put another tomato into her mouth.

"I was thinking…

"Yeah…?"she chewed.

"I guess, right, that maybe ...

She passed the tomato slice to the other side of her mouth and continued chewing. She made a subtle moan of affirmation and raised her eyebrows, encouraging him to continue with the speech.

"I do not know…"

She swallowed the tomato and her face turned red.

"It's just an opinion..."

Lily put her fork down on the table, put her elbow down and dropped her head wearily into the palm of her hand. She watched him lazily, hoping he would stop spinning around.

"That maybe…"

"Get to the point!" She pounded the table, exalted.

Oswald jumped up from the seat, he sat up straight on his back like a soldier.

"You surely know how to get under my skin, God!"she snorted clutching her forehead.

"Okay, okay. Forgive me. I was telling you that I was thinking of buying an incubator.

Lily's eyes widened and she leaned across the table, staring at him; and after a second she laughed out loud like a hyena. Oswald looked at her strangely, he did not understand what was so funny to her, and if she was really doing it in an ironic way, with happiness or if she had thought it was a joke. He, at least, had meant it.

"You're kidding, aren't you, Oswald?

"No. And I don't understand what you're laughing at either.

"I will not put our son inside a wooden box.

"Tell me, then, how you plan to do so, Lily!" He challenged her by opening his arms to the sky, then crossed them and dropped into the chair, waiting for a sensible response. Well... Analyzing how the situation was coming, the only thing he lacked for his wife to tell him was that...

"I'll hatch it, Oswald.

Oswald didn't know what to say. Suddenly he had been paralyzed in the chair with his mind completely blank, like the wall of a psychiatric ward... *Either I admit this crazy woman in a mental hospital*, he thought, *ori will be forced in for going along with her*. Everything disappeared for Oswald in that instant. His body went completely loose. He imagined himself lockedin an infinite room, since there was a ceiling and a floor, but there were no walls to give credit to the total dimensions; there were no shadows, not even his; there was no color, only light. He lay embraced by a strait jacket, sitting cross-legged, balancing delicately, his eyes rolled over and babbling incoherently things he couldn't even hear himself.

Suddenly, he had to shut up after feeling something coming from who-knows- which angle of that great white universe and his eyes forgot that loss to focus on the origin of that sound; though he never stopped balancing.

SILENCE...

Oswald tried to focus and tried to reach far beyond the infinite room, while with his ears, like rabbit ears turning on their axis, he tried to listen to everything that came from his back, with no success...

A deeper silence fell and Oswald tried to concentrate even more. And suddenly a chirp was heard!, which made Oswald go into a state of despair for the echo that formed after that particular sound;he could not notice its origin: it could come from anywhere.

Then he heard a new chirp after about five seconds, then another one and another one immediately after that, and another, and another, and another... as if millions of chicks began to cry looking for their mother, lost, desperate and they ravaged into Oswald's brain, causing greater paranoia. The ground began to vibrate immediately, more and more; and the chirping of an endless number of chicks increased, both in quantity and volume, even reaching a point where they managed to amalgamate and form a single whistle as painful as it was penetrating -like a nail hammered into the leg- maddening; Oswald only wanted to free his arms to cover his ears, he noticed that they were bleeding and that the drops ran like heavy tears, loaded with memories that did not wish to escape. Then, an earthquake; which increased with the hiss. And immediately that hiss materialized in an infinite number of chicks that came running towards Oswald, who went into an even greater restlessness after noticing them approaching at full speed from all directions and shapes. There were chicks that had hatched completely, others that were only eggs with legs, others were approaching rolling since they only had their heads outside the egg, some came with legs and wings outside the shell, others with legs and a head. However, the strangest were the fried eggs with legs and a beak, as well as the boiled eggs, running, and chirping, and saying *DADDY!*

Oswald jumped out of a chair, waking up from his sleep just before the chicks fell on him. Lily looked at him strangely.

"Is something wrong, Oswald?

He just shook his head and continued eating. Lily only served herself salad.

Oswald managed to park in the *Tonietto and Sons* feed store parking lot. There was just one space to do it, so he took advantage of it. Generally, many people went there and it was difficult to find a free spot; Although it had been a long time since he had been going to buy there -to tell the truth, it was Lily who was going to buy millet, birdseed and other seeds at Tonietto's for the different little birds she had in a large cage in the backyard.

Every time he passed by the door with the truck, he saw it packed, even from time to time there was one or two cars disrespectfully double-parked. Probably, the time justified the absence of people. It was only two thirty in the afternoon and *Tonietto and Sons* had continuous opening hours until 7:00 p.m. Lily had sent him to buy a couple of things she needed for their little birds. She said he had already phoned the place and asked old Tonietto to have everything ready for him.

Oswald did not get out of the vehicle immediately. Sitting down, he sighed... somewhat weighed down by the whole morning situation. For a moment, he pressed his eyelids together and longed to wake up from such a nightmare. However, when he opened his eyes again, he found himself sitting inside the truck in the *Tonietto and Sons* parking lot; and sighed a second time...

He got out of the truck and entered the big warehouse. There was no other customer but him. Old Tonietto was behind the counter and, as soon as he saw him, he raised his hand in the air and greeted him:

"Oswald!" He yelled happily. He came around the counter and hurriedly went to hug him. He was limping. "So long, man! What are you doing here?" He grabbed him by the shoulders, squeezing him tightly forcing him to shrug, then met his eyes with a smile. He had known Oswald since he was little. His father used to buy there.

"Good, luckily, Tonietto. You?"

"Good too. Your wife?"

"Good," he said, fragilely doubtful. He didn't know if it was really right or wrong. He smiled anyway, although confused.

"And children? I haven't seen you in years, man! You had some, right?"

"Yes" he thought about Omelette.

"Yes?!" smiling "Congratulations!!"

"HEY, I MEAN NO!!" He interrupted him, quickly correcting himself, understanding that Omelette was an egg and that his wife wasn't there either. "No, no, no."

"Do not?" All the old man's wrinkle son his brows knitted crushing his nose. Oswald had completely and unexpectedly thrown him out of center. "But if your wife, a while ago when she called me, she told me that..."

"Well..." he hesitated shaking his head "yes...", on second thought, the egg was his son.

The old man crossed his arms and looked at him more strangely than usual.

"Well, no!" Oswald exclaimed immediately after feeling that he was getting into his wife's game and that he did not want to go as crazy as she already was. He had to be the sane one, if he wanted to play along.

The old man tightened his arms and focused his gaze on the boy, as if trying to decipher him.

"Well, yeah". He scratched his temple, "technically..." he explained, although it was not entirely explanatory, but even more confusing "yeah... let's say..."

"Do you mean..." he turned his hand in the air as if trying to catch the word that the boy seemed to be unable to spit "that she is pregnant...?"

"Yes!" he answered without giving place for him to continue speaking. "Something like that…"

"Something like that? She told me on the phone that you had a child!"

"Yeah, let's say something like that", he nodded.

"With all due respect, Oswald, I ask you: is the baby yours?"

"Yes..." *I think so...*, he thought to himself as he answered the old man, *Unless Lily is a zoophilic and has not told me anything*, he conjectured in the midst of an internal discord. For a moment, he imagined his wife having sex with a rooster and he must have shaken his head like a dog shakes its body after having gone swimming to get such a pornographically terrifying, chilling and vomiting representation out of his mind. The most pathetic and sad thing about all that aberrant hallucination that had formed in the blink of an eye was that Oswald had imagined entering his bedroom and finding the rooster enjoying his wife and winking at him proudly and victorious. *YUCK!!!* he exclaimed to himself.

The old man grimaced, not being entirely convinced. Then he turned and placed two of his fingers in his mouth to whistle to a boy in the back of the room. When the boy saw him, the old man waved his hand at him. Then he turned to Oswald.

"Roberto will load your order.

Oswald nodded thankfully and asked how much he had to pay as he took out his wallet. When the old man told him how much it was, Oswald said nothing, despite his face of *HOW MUCH???!!!* betrayed him worse than if he had howled like a wounded wolf and Tonietto repeated how much it was; then he saw Roberto pass by with an enormous bag on his shoulder.

"That's broken corn that your wife asked for," said the old man.

Oswald's eyes widened like binoculars, following the entire way of the bag: from the moment he saw Roberto walking through until he disappeared. Then he heard the thud of the bag falling into the box of his pickup F100 and the creaking of the suspension; he understood metaphorically and graphically that this was how the next few days and his wife-as well- would come over him, and that he had to endure all this despite everything, grinding like the pickup shock absorbers.

When he turned to pay, he saw the old man with the little bags of millet and birdseed in his hand. He handed them to Oswald.

"And take this as a gift, man", he said, handing him a smaller bag.

Oswald was grateful although he remained there looking at him, waiting for him to explain what it was.

"They are vitamins for laying hens."

Oswald coughed. He had choked on his own saliva. He thanked him for the gesture, but did not want to accept it. He did not long to have more children, or for his wife to lay more eggs, or to have children shaped like eggs, or eggs shaped like a son, or for his wife to cook an egg for him that she laid, or to buy eggs, or salad with potato, mayonnaise and egg, or… ENOUGH! HE DIDN'T KNOW WHAT HE WANTED OR WHAT HE HAD! ALL THIS MESS ABOUT THE EGG WOULD END UP WITH HIM IN A MADHOUSE!

The old man insisted anyway, and Oswald had to accept the bag of vitamins.

He did not understand how he managed to drive home. He only remembered getting into the truck at the gate of the forage and having it started; then a blink and he was at home getting out of the vehicle with the bag of vitamins in hand. Although he knew the way perfectly, all its colours, smells and shapes, he remembered absolutely nothing of this last trip. His mind had gone back travelling like that interface during lunch, though this time while driving; he could only remember broken eggs, legs, chickens, and shells. Oswald couldn't think of anything else but hallucinating about everything that was happening fantastically and chillingly in his life. He didn't understand whether it was a miracle from Heaven or a nightmare from Hell; or a nightmare from Heaven or a miracle from Hell!

Finding himself already with the bag in hand under the F100, he curiously glanced at the vitamins there dangling between his fingers and knew immediately that he should hide it where Lily could not find it. He didn't want his wife to eat them like a box of addictive *Kellogg's* cereal and start laying eggs everywhere. And then suddenly came up with a place where Lily would never find her!

"LOVE!" Lily appeared rounding the corner of the gallery.

Oswald, taken by surprise, turned quickly and tried to throw the bag of vitamins into the truck and close the door immediately. He would come looking for it later to hide it. Immediately he turned on his axis, turned back to Lily, and leaned against the truck so that she had no room to open it, nor would it occur to her to do so.

"Have you brought everything?" she asked as she advanced towards him.

"Yes..." he replied, looking at her strangely: the dress that Lily was wearing had thrown him off, "my love...

The girl was dressed in her wedding attire: a long, white floor-length skirt extending from her hips fell like a cascading of waterfall as sweet as it was flimsy; from the waist upwards, a singular blouse with shoulder pads. She was wearing no jewellery, no gloves, and she was barefoot. But the most peculiar thing of all, although she had no crown, she wore instead a red-dyed glove like a harlequin's hat, with the five fingers falling to one side as if it were ... *A CREST!* Oswald exclaimed to himself, *OH MY GOD!* It was a very strong image. Shocking!

She kissed him.

Oswald had the intention of asking her what she was doing dressed like this, although he tried to keep quiet so as not to start a new argument and, on top of that, lose out on who knows how many disputes he had lost that day.

He followed her as she turned and walked to the house. At that moment he felt like a chick following its mother, searching the ground for some lost seed or grain; however, his head was down as he was thinking what he would do next, how all this madness would continue and in what way and to what extent he should and could play along with his wife. He felt himself completely gone. At one point he raised his looked upas he noticed another strange attitude in Lily -although, by the way, not so strange because of how everything was evolving- and he saw her trying to scratch the ground with her feet, gently stirring the earth as if looking for some earthworm. However, she did not crouch or anything like that, she simply made such a gesture as if on a nervous impulse and continued walking. Oswald stopped for such an instant to stare in amazement at the situation. He was stunned for a moment and then resumed his stride after subtly shaking his head.

They entered the house and Oswald put the bags on the counter. He looked delicately at everything around him and was *glad* enough that everything was in order: but he did not know if taking this as suspicious...

"Have you brought the corn?" Lily asked as she approached the kitchen to finish cooking a stew. She took the wooden spoon and began to stir it. She looked at her husband as she did so.

He nodded with a smile and, as he took out the things he had bought out of the bag, added:

"Yes, it's in the back of the truck" he did a pause briefly, until he decided that what he was going to say next should be somewhat softer and not so direct. "Mr. Tonietto ordered a large bag to be loaded".

"Yes", Lily answered flatly, having understood where her husband's words were coming from, so she added a sharp look but also with the same subtle tone he had towards her; anyway, it came out more ironic than anything else. "I asked him. Is there a problem with it?"

"No, no, my love."

"Ah…" she arched her eyebrows and continued stirring the stew. The glove that served as her crest moved to the other side.

A slightly awkward silence followed.

"Omelette?" Oswald asked as he stepped into the dining room after walking around the breakfast bar that divided it from the kitchen. He stood for a moment looking for the egg in every corner with his gaze.

"Sleeping," Lily answered.

I didn't know that eggs were sleeping now!, he exclaimed to himself, *this is the last straw!* However, the only thing he could think to say from his mouth was:

"I don't see it, my love.

"It's in our room," she answered and left the kitchen.

Oswald turned his eyes to his right. The bedroom door was closed, however the small gap between it and the floor gave a glimpse of something not quite common... -or, let's say, curious... PECULIAR!- escaping like confetti. Such was the peculiarity of it, like everything else that had been happening lately -something that Oswald firmly hoped was a nightmare- that he could not believe that his wife had left the house.

Drawn by the discomfort of the mismatch between what should be and what it really was, or also between what he prayed it wasn't and what definitely WAS, he walked towards it. Such a sensation possessed more force than a magnet; even more force than gravity, so that the fact of going to his bedroom did not correspond to his simple will, but rather that he was constrained by the tension.

When he reached the door, he stopped. Placing his hands on the handles, gently pushed them and they opened wide softly as well. He didn't want to think about fried eggs -he didn't even want to think about eggs or anything that was shaped like that!- but his eyes widened as such on a frying pan that could cook up to six of them at once and without touch each other. The room was absolutely covered in...

"Sawdust!" He translated his thought into words when he saw the bedroom invaded by all those pieces of wood. The floor was not visible; it was a carpet of chopped-up wood. The bed was also covered by them and on it, *sleeping*, was Omelette. Although it wasn't all! Above the bed, just inches above, across the room from side to side, a thick and long branch of a tree laid supported by one of the shelves in the closet and the window.

It was a moment when he didn't know whether to laugh, cry, run away, or jump all over the sawdust carpet and start playing like a child in a pool of plastic balls. Until at one point he decided to step into the bedroom and confirm whether, indeed, it was about sawdust or not -despite the fact that he already knew 100% that it was not necessary to do so.

"It's beautiful how he sleeps, isn't it?!"

Oswald jumped immediately. His wife had appeared him from behind, making him come back from the astonishment in which he had plunged. With his hand on his chest and catching his breath, he turned to say:

"Oh, Lily! You scared me... WHAT ARE YOU EATING?!" He interrupted himself when he saw her chewing and with a bag in her hand filled with some colourful...

"Ah! A bag that I found on the top of the truck" she answered immediately with a friendly smile.

Oswald leaned against the door to keep from falling. He wasn't feeling well.

"Can you hold it, please?" Lily handed him the bag of vitamins. Oswald grabbed it. "Put them there for me", she pointed to a cabinet in the kitchen, "I'll eat them in the afternoon. Now I'm going to take a nap with my child.

Then Lily went into the bedroom and climbed onto the bed —she didn't use her hands to help herself, by the way. Oswald watched her intently from his awkward, near-fainting position, the bag of vitamins dangling from his fingers and visualizing himself surrounded by more and more eggs. Lily walked across the bed to the pole and jumped when she found herself in front of him and gripped with both feet. She shook his body and snuggled up. She closed his eyes and fell asleep.

Oswald closed the door and went outside to get some air. He needed it.

Lying for a while in the Paraguayan hammock brought a little peace to his life that afternoon. He did not know how many hours he had slept; he was simply full of joy and it was enough. Hearing the birds singing and soaring through the air, as well as smelling the eucalyptus scent of the trees from which the hammock hung was like splashing in a tub of gold coins or bathing in champagne.

He heard footsteps approaching, followed by Lily's voice asking him:

"Wouldyou join us for tea?"

Oswald noticed immediately that Lily had Omelette cuddled in her hands and against her chest. By the way, she hadn't taken off that ridiculous chicken costume she'd made for herself. The glove continued to swing from side to side above her head.

"Yes, for sure," Oswald replied and got up. The concrete table with marble decorations next to it already had a kettle ready. So there were also bowls with various grains, a packet of rice crackers and a jar of jam.

Lily placed the egg in a small wicker bowl and served the tea next.

"What will you cook tonight, love?" Oswald asked, spreading jam on one of the rice crackers.

"What would you like me to make?" she asked while taking a handful of corn and put it in his mouth.

In an instant, Oswald believed she would break not one but several teeth.

"A tor… WHAT ARE YOU DOING!?" the man frowned his bow to the point where all his wrinkles were conglomerated towards the end of his nose; in turn, he shook his head and gestured with his hands, spinning them incongruously in the air a turn or two-

"SH!!!" Lily quickly silenced him, and immediately whispered, "Shut up.

Lily was looking at the ground. Mindfully. Her eyes were fixed and her pupils seemed to chase in a tiny way, with almost imperceptible, searching, mad-scientist movements, something that was moving there.

And suddenly she stopped and Oswald was startled, falling backwards from the concrete bench that surrounded the table! Lily stood up and scratched the ground with her bare feet. Her hands were lying on his waist and his elbows had begun to flap. Until, in the blink of an eye, she reached down and took a worm in her mouth. She sat up in a jiffy and stretched her neck to the sky with the worm dancing between his lips. She made some extravagant movements with her head as she sucked on the worm like spaghetti in the *Lady and the Tramp movie* in the famous kiss scene.

Oswald observed the movements of his wife with his mouth open and was glad to be on the ground, otherwise, he would have fallen again... He noticed how the annelid struggled to live to the point that Oswald believed that it would grow legs like centipedes and he would somehow run faster than a hare fleeing from some hunter. He watched as the Adam's apple, clearly and utterly overlooked by the women, was going up and down on Lily with a mad frenzy like a broken elevator.

Lily didn't reply. Suddenly she stopped chewing and stared at him. Oswald did not understand why.

"Can you repeat please?"

"What... what... what?" he stammered, in puzzlement.

"What do you want me to make you for dinner?" She asked as she sat down on the bench again.

"Leave it! Don't do anything!" He quickly denied, straightening up and brushing some of the dust off his pants. "I'll buy some pizzas", he said as he walked away to go to the bathroom.

"Don't you think we'd better go out for dinner?

"No, my love, I'll get some pizzas.

On the way home, Oswald had called Lily to tell her he was getting the pizzas and to *please* set the table. He explained that he had bought two: one with ham and bell peppers and the other with ham and pineapple.

In the midst of it and somewhat enthusiastic, he proposed to open one of those bottles of wine that they had saved to celebrate special occasions. However, on the other side he heard his wife to say that she wasn't really feeling well to drink a toast, that she felt uncomfortable, upset as if something in her ovaries was bothering her. Oswald was thoughtful and, although it did not completely collapse, he perceived his enthusiasm melted like a painting by Dalí.

He traveled with one of the vehicle's lights flashing to shortly fade out. *I'll have to go to the mechanic any minute*, he thought. He got to the house and parked the truck in front of the door. He got out and went to the nose of the F100 to check how the light was working and reaffirmed what he had thought minutes ago, adding that it would be a danger to continue driving in such conditions. He returned to the booth, turned off the lights, and grabbed the pizzas with one hand; with the other he reached into his pocket for the keys. He reached the door and opened it announcing that he had already arrived. He noticed that the table was not set and Lily was not there she had not answered him either.

"LILY?!" he insisted as he placed the pizzas on the table. He saw Omelette placed in a cardboard box surrounded by a matted sawdust mattress and a lamp giving it heat.

There was the sound of the toilet flushing.

"Lily?!" Oswald asked again, leaning out into the corridor. "Are you okay?!

Lily appeared holding her lower abdomen. She still hadn't taken off that white dress and the ridiculous glove she wore on her head.

"Oh, love, sorry... When you called me I was in the bathroom, I couldn't do anything you asked me to do.

"Are you in any pain?

"The ovaries, I suppose, I have just had some leakage. I just went for a pee and I think there is something wrong", she said, complaining a little, like grumbling, and leaning with one of his hands against a wall while with the other she continued stroking the one below the navel.

"Let's go to the doctor urgently!" He took her by the wrist with force.

"No!" She jerked away. "I do not want to!"

"But..." He tried to grab her again.

"NO"she dodged her hand "IT'S *NO* AND ENOUGH!" She glared at him.

"Very well... whatever you want..." He raised his hands to his ears and shrugged. Then he turned and, going to the cupboard to get some plates and glasses, added, "It's up to you."

Lily sat down at the table next to Omelette; She put the heat lamp aside and began to caress him gently while muttering something unintelligible to Oswald in baby language. Oswald, for now, approached with the utensils and distributed them on the table. He had also picked up a large blade in case the pizza was not well cut -it always happened-. He opened one of the boxes -the one containing the ham and bell peppers- and immediately began to go over the lines that delimited the portions with the edge of the knife. In some he heard the tasty *CRACK* of a base made perfectly toof stone. He then served one to his wife. She thanked.

"I think Omelette will have a little sister..." she said after swallowing the first piece she had bitten and chewed.

Oswald had not even finished cutting the first slice of pizza with his teeth, that the shock caused by such news made his chocking breath suck up such a piece like a vacuum cleaner and get stuck on his epiglottis. He immediately stood up, pushing the chair back with his legs out of inertia, and spat the chunk out with greater power than if he had fired a Wild West revolver. It fell right in front of his wife's eyes, who was stunned for a moment watching the small fraction of pizza... then she looked up, while with both hands she covered the opposite sides of the egg that she had laid -as if it had ears and she wanted to cover them so that Omellette would not hear what she was going to say next-, to which she said angrily and indignantly:

"Is that how you insult our son?!

He was stunned for a moment with his hand on his throat.

"Is that how you respond to the desire to give Omelette a sister?!

"Lil," he hesitated, "... Lily, I was suffocating... Please!"

"Is this how you express the love you have for your children?!" she continued without crediting him.

"Please, Lily, don't be ridiculous!" He waved his hand in the air angrily, although really more than anger, it was confusion,"How do you think...?!

"RIDICULOUS?!" She interrupted him by standing up abruptly, leaning on the table, leaning hauntingly and her eyes enormously like saucers. Her pupils focused on her husband as if they wanted to set him on fire.

"Calm down, please, Lily!" He exclaimed as he took the chair back to sit down and continue eating.

She simply followed him penetratingly with her intense pupils as she breathed furiously. Her nostrils flared and contracted frantically.

"How do you think I won't like the idea of having another boy or girl?!" He sat. "Simply, the news has taken me by surprise."

"Are you serious?" Lily's voice had completely transmuted: in a second she had gone from being the devil himself in the middle of an exorcism to an angel swinging on a swing in the middle of a square full of children.

Oswald understood that Lily's cyclothymic complex was due to her hormonal disorder -or at least he wanted to understand that it was that way-. And what a mess! She had laid an egg!

"And what a surprise!" exclaimed the man and raised his eyebrows and smiled without showing his teeth. He picked up the slice of pizza again to continue eating.

"Ooooohhhhh," his wife sighed deeply, as if conquered by a perfume of love and tenderness, like those air fresheners with names like *Cotton Clouds*, *Peach Diapers* or *Baby Caresses*. The only thing missing was that the *Pumpkin Porridge Poop* came out... "You're a sweet..." she added as she sat down again. Then she extended her hands over the table, palms up, encouraging him to hand over his. She smiled at him as her eyes glazed over.

Oswald put the pizza aside and smiled back. He grabbed his wife's hands and... and... were they his wife's hands? He was surprised. Again, while she wasn't startled, she did stifle a small hiccup in silence, trying to past his emotions somewhat unnoticed. Fortunately, he didn't have another piece of pizza in his mouth, otherwise he would have choked and spit it out again. He had noticed her skin rougher than normal.

Lily was one to use creams, essentially on her hands, and it was one of the things about Lily that Oswald fell in love with: her hands. To tell the truth, her caresses. She had such a soft and velvety caress that she managed to lead anyone to contemplate the immensity of the universe in the depths of himself. Each caress allowed a journey of introspection to all tenderness. However, he couldn't feel the same now. He understood that his wife, due to this madness of believing herself a hen after... *giving birth? Give birth to an egg?* Oswald found himself absolutely confused, *laying Omelette? Booh! Anyway!* This madness of believing herself to be a hen had led her to stop taking care of her skin, which is why she got chicken-skin, clearly, one hundred percent. *Or more than a hundred?!*, exclaimed the man, opening his eyes widely, astonished, when his fingertips noticed more than goose bumps, but some feathers next to small elevations that seemed to be tiny calamus, which in the future would support the feathers already formed.

Oswald slept that night on the sofa. Entering into the bedroom was basically impossible. Lily had managed to make it a far more authentic chicken coop than the day before. There were branches everywhere, sawdust on top of the bed and the floor, a large pizza plate where she put cracked corn and other grains... and even all of that had already spread to the living room, so in the blink of an eye Lily would culminate transforming her house into a chicken coop. From head to toe. From floor to ceiling.

Oswald jumped up the next morning when he heard his wife singing -okay, trying to sing! since some of her husky human voice mixed with some morning phlegm-. So her singing was out of tune like a rooster in the room at 6 o'clock in the morning, barely the first ray of light filtered through the crack of the low blind. Although he woke up somewhat shocked, he was not entirely surprised: he knew that something like this would come sooner or later, essentially after noticing the night before that Lily had started to grow real feathers!

So he took it as normal, at least then he would have to accept it! What's more, when he saw her get off one of the poles that crossed the bedroom from side to side, with her hands in fists placed on her waist, with her elbows pointing outwards, forming the vertex of an isosceles triangle –consisting of her arm, forearm and latissimus dorsi- and moving them in a useless flapping, he heard in his left ear a kind of invisible gnome advising him: *Well, yes... resign yourself, man...*

Oswald sighed deeply, although certainly that had more burden of resignation as such –and subsequent acceptance, he thought he assumed at least– than anything else. Truth be told, Lily's transformation into a hen, which had started out as a kind of insanity, according to him, but had turned into the real thing, was progressing faster than his mind could allow him to accept the situation; so -he thought more confidently- he was honestly going through a process of resignation. What was the difference back then between resigning and accepting? That he would still go along with his wife -*yes, RESIGNATION!* he said to himself-, believing that everything was still a fantasy putting upside down the whole bedroom -and notoriously in the future the house!- as a chicken coop, acting like a hen, dressing like one of it and *blah, blah, blah…* was playing with Oswald's mind. *But how was it possible the barbs of a feather thing?*, an invisible gnome asked in his ear. *Bullshit!*, replied the boy, *I am wrong, my mind is wrong! I'm starting to hallucinate!*, he continued to respond to that voice that he should know where it came from -actually, he knew that it was from his mind but it seemed to be outside- *She's making me hallucinate!*, he added when Lily came out of the bedroom and walked past him. *And what is that on her feet?!*, asked the little voice. Oswald observed carefully: they had grown dewclaws!

"Good morning my love!" Lily greeted happily as she passed him.

Oswald did not reply. He hadn't heard her. His pupils had been frozen at the point where he had seen his wife's spurs a few seconds ago.

"Good morning my love!" Lily repeated when she didn't hear his answer and turned to see what was wrong with him. "Oswald?!"

He didn't answer her. He did not hear her. He was ... ABSORBED!

"Oswald!" Lily exclaimed again after taking him by the shoulder and shaking him. She noticed that he jumped, scared. "Is something wrong with you? Are you okay?

The man nodded with a weak *yes*, which came out of his mouth as if it were a swift blow, accompanied by a movement of his head. He settled on the sofa.

"I'll make breakfast, okay?" Lily said, giving him a subtle pat on the back.

"Yes, yes ..." He spat them out again in a breath.

"Very well..." she said, turned and walked away to the kitchen.

Oswald took the opportunity to look at Lily's ankles again as she retired to the kitchen to see if he had really seen what he had seen. And yes, he had seen it! He had seen them! They were small, but there they were: ONE. IN. EACH. FOOT. And he dropped his face into his hands, clutched his forehead and kneaded it like stomach walls move the food inside to digest it as best as possible, so that his brain could do the same with the images he had just captured from the feet of his wife.

Finally, he took a deep breath and got up from the couch. He placed his hands on his hips and thought for a few moments as he contemplated his bedroom, which had become a chicken coop, about to expand throughout the house with the force of a supernova explosion. At that moment he decided that the best thing to do would be to build a chicken coop outside the house.

Unexpectedly, the doorbell rang, just as Oswald's bladder was ringing at the door, wanting to deflate. He had barely started his walk to the bathroom when he had to turn and look out the window. He could see at the end of the gravel path that connected the house with the door that led to the street a short silhouette with a very particular coral-colored cartwheel hat. She was also wearing a rosewood pink shawl and pale pink shorts. She was wearing modern cherry red tennis shoes. The silhouette insisted on the bell once more.

"Who is it, Oswald?" Lily asked from the kitchen.

"Mom ..." he answered nervously. "I don't know what she wants at this hour" said while going to the kitchen to take the keys and open the door. "I haven't even had time to go to the bathroom.

"Ah! I called her yesterday", she pointed out and put some water to boil. She'd make tea, clearly. There were already three tea bags in three different cups next to the cooker. She was already expecting her, clearly. "I have told her about Omelette".

Oswald glared at her after taking the keys. He was in a jumble. He watched her silently, waiting for her to continue with some further explanation.

"Okay, okay..." She sighed with a renegade jerk and rolled his eyes. She clarified: "Calm down! I simply told her that we had a beautiful surprise that we wanted to announce to her, something that she had been yearning for a long time.

"Did you tell her that you laid an egg?!

"You don't hear me, do you?" She insisted, shaking his head with a certain wearisome air. "I told her we had a surprise". At that moment the doorbell rang again. "Nothing more. And I have invited her to have breakfast. Now go and open the door".She indicated the door with a slight movement of his chin. Then she turned and walked away saying, "I'll go to the bathroom in the meantime."

"Good, but be quick," her husband warned her. "Once I open it to my mother, I need to use it urgently", he put his hand under his belly.

Oswald left the house and went to the barred door. He greeted his mother on the drive down the gravel path.

"Are you peeing yourself?" asked the mother disgustingly, noticing his step between hurried and tight, almost brushing their knees against each other with each step.

"You haven't even given me time to go to the bathroom," he said as he tried to insert the key into the hole in the grate. "I just got up" The *damn* key in the lock had become an impossible mission to accomplish. "What do you bring in the bag?" He was curious when he saw that she was trying to hide something behind his skinny legs.

"Something for my future grandson..."she smiled mischievously, giggling and blushing "... or granddaughter..." At that very moment the key *clicked*. The woman entered and greeted her son with a kiss on the cheek while placing the palm of one of her hands on the opposite cheek. She patted him softly, proud and joyful. She added as she did so,"Congratulations! You and Lily will tell me about it..."

Yes, he said to himself, sighing somewhat confused, *we'll tell you about it...*

Then there was a loud sound and the woman was startled. It came from inside the house, she supposed, or from the back of the park. It had been a familiar sound, broken, although it slightly dissonant pitch, as it mixed a certain tone of human joy with that of a bird. *Neither very, very, nor so, so.* It was not quite a definite sound. It was amorphous, a bizarre mixture of a human trying to sing a Whitney Houston song for the first time with aberrant results, bordering on a giant mammal in heat in some Canadian forest. The lady tried to guess:

"Is that a giant hen..."she looked at his son with his eyes wide, big and pointing with her left index finger up, shaking it delicately to the rhythm of her ironic intonation "or your neighbor, the crazy one in the background, signed up for classes singing songs with Ricardo, The Baker?

Everyone in town knew that Ricardo, The Baker was the worst singer in town. Nevertheless, he believed that he sang well, by the way. Anyone who went to his store to shop, was received with the music that Ricardo, The Baker made proliferate from his vocal cords with enthusiasm so that his customers could take a smile with them. However, his singing was sad and hurt anyone's ears. The legend tells -or rather, Ricardo, The Baker tells, or rather, has told and has spread throughout the city! (currently and without a doubt, it is used for all jokes for having)- that Ricardo, The Baker had been a great singer but that his voice was never the same when one day he had been cornered by his own canaries and the next day he woke up lying on the floor unable to speak. As time went by, he recovered his voice, but Ricardo, The Baker could no longer sing as he did before. The legend points out that the little birds had hatched a revenge and organized a plot. They were fed up with hearing Ricardo, The Baker sing over his songs every day and almost every moment that he was in the house. Ricardo, The Baker has pointed out, on the contrary, that for him it was envy -nevertheless, most of the people, adhere more to the story of being fed up-.

Ricardo, The Baker has affirmed that the birds were bothered by the beauty of his voice, and that is why they attacked him, *they could not bear to be overthrown,* said with hatred Ricardo, The Baker, who had begun to hate canaries from that day on.

Truth be told, from that day on, he never had another bird in his house as a pet. Beyond all the mixed feelings... the canaries cornered him and attacked him when Ricardo, The Baker, went to get them out of the small room where he kept them at night, and who knows what spell they did on him or what else. Anyway... the point was that Ricardo, The Baker was the worst singer in town.

"Have you bought chickens?" Oswald's mother insisted consistently, scowling at him.

The sound that had been heard was manifestly a deep, loud, uncoordinated clucking.

"Because that was as if a hen laid a BIIIIIIIIIG egg," said the old woman, opening her eyes like bottle butts as she pronounced the *I's*. She seemed exalted.

"Uh..." He hesitated. "No, no... I*(we)*'ll tell you" He did not express the *we* outwards, but rather thought it after the image of Lily laying another egg came to him.

"OSVAAAAAAAAAAAALD!!!" His wife appeared shouting and running with such joy that it filled her husband with chills.

Lily was holding something in his hands and the boy suspected what it was, essentially after what had happened the night before.

Oswald's mother (Irene, by the way, her name), put her hand to her chest after feeling that she had run out of air when she saw her appear with all that homemade costume. He immediately gave a quick glance to his son, who returned it with some pity, as if apologizing, and returned it to his daughter-in-law... well, to tell the truth, basically she looked at the red glove she was wearing on her head as if it would be a hen crest! It was moving back and forth, without absolute coordination at all.

"Hello Irene!" she exclaimed with a smile that at that moment frightened the old woman.

"Hello..." She made a pause and took the opportunity to smile doubtfully after the *shock*. She took a deep breath and concluded, "Lily!" She kissed her cheek.

"I understand that this may seem a bit..." Lily continued.

"Weird?" Irene quickly interposed.

Lily didn't like her using that word very much and tried to hide her disgust, however, she couldn't quite, manage it.

"*Not entirely natural*, I'd rather you said," Oswald's wife replied.

"Miracle?" Irene corrected herself.

"Yes! That's what I would call it!" she pointed out fervently with enthusiasm and a smile where the corners of his mouth seemed to be about to reach his temples"Right?" She looked at Oswald. "What do you think?! Miracle, right?!"

He simply nodded.

"Well, that's how she will be called..." She showed what she had cuddled up against her chest: she extended his arms and opened his hands. Another egg. "Miracle!"

Irene gaped at the egg.

"Lily, you still don't know if it will be a girl," Oswald pointed out.

"I know!" The woman broke in with withering fury almost above his words, also giving him a devilish look. Although she immediately returned her pupils to the egg and her altered hormones immediately acted, so she said as sweetly as an angel: "She is my daughter!"

At that moment, Irene collapsed on her back.

She noticed her eyes throbbing and she began to blink slightly. Slowly she opened her eyes and her pupils got used to a powerful white light that annoyingly dazzling her. To her left she heard the electronic chirping to the rhythm of her heart'spumping. Turning her head there, she observed a small television transmitting a black background with a green line running from left to right, which to the beat of the same robotic chirping destabilized the drawn straight line, going up, then down, and then joining again the same of the previous straight line; and again going up and down and rejoined it.

"What the hell..." she blasphemed as she continued to contemplate her situation, dumbfounded. Then she noticed a kind of mechanical coat rack from which hung a bag filled with serum, from which a very thin hose was detached, which was connected to her body through a hypodermic needle "... is this shit!" She ended when she saw the left wrist with the needle inserted.

Irene turned her head to the other side and saw her son, sleeping sitting in an armchair, all hunched over and his head bowed. She considered that he would get up with an unbearable contracture in his neck.

"Oswald!" she yelled at him and repeated with greater vehemence when she noticed that she hadn't moved a hair: "Oswald! OSWALD!"

The boy leaped to his feet, as if he were a man who had regained his breath after he had given him mouth-to-mouth resuscitation and brought him back to life. He seemed to have woken up from a nightmare. He had been dreaming that he wanted to eat something, although the only thing he had in his fridge were eggs -indeed, this topic was overwhelming him!- that Lily had laid; in addition, some ham and cheese as well. So, he had decided to prepare an omelette. The crucial point in the story was when each time he grabbed an egg and was about to break it, it would come out legs, or a beak, or wings, or a nose, or legs, or arms... and suddenly *Oswald!* the frightening cry of Lily and him trying to flee without knowing where while looking for the perfect excuse in case his wife found out, *Oswald! OSV...*

"... VALD!" his mother woke him up.

"Mother!" He shook his head and approached the bed. "Are you feeling okay?"

"Yes! Thanks!" she said with some sarcasm as she tried to sit up. Her son helped her with a button, which adjusted the backrest. "Can you get me out of this fucking chloroform-smelling place?"

Oswald took a deep breath. He did not reply.

"What happened? Why am I here? How long have I been like this? What... what... what... WHAT THE HELL?!" She slapped her fists on the bed angrily.

Oswald trembled. He got scared. Yes. He had been frightened to the point that he had gritted his teeth, remembering such blasphemy when his mother whipped him around with the slipper, the sneaker, or whatever was on his feet. It flew across the entire house, side to side, and struck Oswald's bedroom door just in time when he, after a run like a drug dealer short of bullets shooting out of a gunfight, slammed it shut after cross the threshold.

Oswald hesitated for a moment to tell her the truth. He did not know if in such a situation it would be good for her. Perhaps it would be convenient to make it up. Anyway, she didn't remember what had happened! And forget the *Omelette topic* for later ...

"Lily laid an egg, right?!" she asked harshly, looking tenaciously into his eyes.

Okay. She had remembered. There was no room to lie to her, then. Truth be told, it had been two eggs! However, Oswald simply refrained from nodding his head. Irene then looked to the side and added, shaking her head:

"I thought it was over..."

Oswald was surprised. He said nothing. He stared into the emptiness, his eyes focused on any point in the room. Then he felt his mother grasp his hands and cup them gently in hers, as if capturing a cottony dandelion with its cyselas yearning to detach itself and fly away with an ethereal breeze. Oswald looked at Irene's hands and then at her. Irene focused on their hands. Her eyes were glassy while she was trying to hide in them an irrepressible anguish, which began to unleash in a sick trembling of his throat trying to tie itself. She kept in silence...

It was difficult for her to look up and face her son when he asked her what was wrong. Every time she tried to do so, she must have returned her gaze to her hands to keep from bursting into tears. She grimaced with her mouth in all directions to avoid letting out her cracking voice. She wanted to get herself under control before speaking, something Oswald quickly realized: his mother always did the same. Then he picked up the glass of water that was lying on the side and handed it to her. His mother took it and drank. She drank it all, in one go. She felt the water fill her chest, hardening it like lead, so it helped hold back the crying. Then she sighed deeply and broke the silence by repeating:

"I thought it was over."She put the glass down in the same place where his son had taken it and again brought her hands to wrap his son's.

"That It had finished what, Mom."

Irene dared to look him in the eyes. Deeply. She bit his lip, swallowed hard, and exclaimed seriously:

"The avian revolution.

Oswald chuckled and asked:

"What are you talking about?!"

"The Revenge of the chickens.

Oswald cupped his forehead with both hands and, while covering his face, wrinkled it and massaged his eyes with the heels of his hands. He clearly wanted to wake up from that nightmare of beaks and feathers urgently. He was hesitant to have really woken up. He still believed he had awakened from a dream within the dream, so he continued to be asleep... *right?,* he hesitated.

"Please, Mom!" He returned his hands to hers.

"Shut up and listen!" She interrupted him quickly, giving him a palm on one of his hands.

Very good, he told himself. He was silent and he would listen. Then he would wake up... *or am I already awake?*

Irene began her narration:

"Everything happened when I was a child ...

Oswald frowned.

"On the farm where we lived with your grandparents..." She sighed, shaking his head after beginning to remember. "It was my turn to go to collect the eggs in the henhouse like every day. Dad told me to collect everything" it was at the time of the story where Irene began to accompany it with gestures of her hands. Oswald knew from the beginning that she would not hold them back for the whole story. "Absolutely everything. Even if the hens were brooding, to pick them up by the tail –she gestured with her right hand as if she were picking her up and removing with her left hand taking away the eggs she sat on– and take them away ALL the eggs they had.

>> However, one day like any other, on my way to get the eggs" she pointed her index finger firmly at the ceiling; her pupils had been strongly positioned in the right angle of her eyes remembering something with integrity, "the feeling was not the same" she shook her head lightly and frantically and changed her tone of voice to something more ghostly "... The hens were already looking at me evilly."

"They looked at you badly," he pointed out... with a certain irony. To which he repeated with pauses and in the same tone, inclining his head and looking at her from the side, his eyes narrowed suspiciously: "The hens... looked at you... badly. Did I understand well?

Irene widened her eyes and nodded her head without hesitation. Oswald let her continue with the story.

"I got into the chicken coop with a certain suspicion that something was not right in my first steps. But I didn't want to give it too much importance so as not to scare me. You know how I am when I become skeptical ...

"Yes, your nerves" Oswald confirmed with a nod of his head.

"Well, but not everything!" the old woman quickly contradicted him with a frown.

"Ghosts..." he sighed annoyed as he thought about other things that made his mother nervous. He continued counting: "strange things... new things... the future," he began to do a list when he remembered discovering her going to the woman who threw cards at him. And he looked at her inclining his head slightly, knowingly, when she said about the future.

"Just once I have gone to Cecilia to read my future through the cards!" She quickly stepped defensively.

"Mother!" he complained annoyed.

"Well, well, two or three!" she corrected herself. "But no more!

"And the hand reading at María Inés?!" Oswald reminded her.

"I went once!" She raised his index finger to highlight that had clearly gone once.

"And the reading of the coffee grounds at Clotilde's?!

The old woman snorted annoyed through her nose, rolled her eyes and bit her lip. She moved her mouth everywhere.

"Ah! And the hand reading at Ana María's?!" He continued, adding as they came to mind.

"I insist! Ana María does not read hands!" she exclaimed angrily. The sound of the electronic device signaling cardiac activity was heard to increase its rhythm immaculately. Although it had already been on the rise since her son had begun to expose all his truths, at that moment she was more agitated than necessary. "Ana María is *doing* hands! She *does* hands!" she emphasized with fervor, showing him her nails; and repeated once more: "She did my hands! Paint the nails!" She explained.

"What difference does it make! You always came back nervous from those places!"

"Because Ana María always does my hands a mess!"

Oswald was silent for a moment. He shook his head and added, puzzled, with a certain stutter:

"And for... what were you going for?!" Immediately he corrected himself, since his mother was still going there: "What are you going for?!"

"Ana María is my friend! And while we talk, we have tea and she enjoys painting my nails! And while I do not like how she paints them, she is my friend and full stop! It makes her happy! Old people's stuff! Period! Shit!" She hit the mattress with her fists.

"Okay ... Let's forget this. The chicken coop, please!" located it in time and space.

"Ah! Yes! I went into the chicken coop and discovered that something was wrong with the hens. They looked at me weird. They were making strange noises" she narrowed her eyes and her voice became somewhat terrifying "their cackles were gloomy and little by little they were amplified with each step I made. And at one point they began to surrounded me" from distant points, at medium speed, she was bringing her hands in a C-shape until they were joined by her fingers, fingertips to fingertips, enclosing the air. "The hens in front of me began to approach and joined the hens behind me a little more than halfway across the henhouse. I stayed still. I thought if I took one more step, they would pounce on me. Then I saw in the distance the glare of eyes, which immediately jumped from the darkness of the enclosure tothe end of the coop where the hens laid their eggs, extended its delicate and feathery limbs to cushion its landing and stood in front of me with its slender and beautiful figure..." Irene described him as if she was melting with love at that moment.

She paused.

Oswald noticed how his mother's eyes blazed with passion and flickered as if she had been enchanted by a potion of adoration.

"Your father," she finished with a sigh of intensely deep love.

Oswald swallowed hardly. He wanted to faint... HE FAINTED!

Oswald slowly half-opened his eyes. Above him he had three faces that were watching him curiously. One of them pointed a light to his eyes and pronounced something he did not understand. However, he could read his lips very well, so he replied while holding his head with one hand and helping him to get up off the ground with the other:

- Yes, I'm OK. Thanks.

The doctors said something else that Oswald did not quite hear, he was still feeling somewhat dazed, and they handed him a glass of water.

"Thank you." He handed the glass back to them and stood up. A doctor held out his hand and he took it. She stammered something else, yet all he understood was... *something else?* to which he replied, "No, thank you, I'm fine. I'll sit here again." He leaned back in the chair near his mother's bed.

- Rrrr... emberrr... what happened?" said another of the doctors. He didn't quite understand it, but the words became clearer and clearer. *Piano piano* he was stabilizing himself.

"Yes, something..." He sat down and looked at his mother, who was looking at him somewhat dumb founded. "I was thrilled to hear my mother talk about my father", he muttered.

"You fainted!" Irene said with her peculiar voice and opening her eyes widening. That voice he had heard clearly.

He nodded with a wry smile and said after a quick snort of his nose:

"Oh, don't tell me!" Then he turned to the doctors: "I'm fine, thank you. I would need to speak to my mother alone."

"If you need anything, call us, okay?" one of them said, clapping him on the shoulder. Then the three of them left the room and closed the door behind them.

Irene and her son exchanged a few silent glances without really knowing who had to start talking: whether she should continue to tell her magical story or he should ask. The situation was honestly a bit uncomfortable until such an atmosphere was broken when Oswald sighed loudly as he returned to cup his mother's hands in his, which gave her the confidence to continue with her story.

"Please continue," he said.

Irene bit her lips. She looked at the window. She took a deep breath. Deep down through her nose. She looked at his son again and blew out her breath. She continued:

- Your father looked at me from the compound, jumped and flew to me. He was a beautiful *singing Berger*, the greatest I had ever seen. His black color speckled with gold..."she began to describe it with an extraordinary radiance both in the timbre of her voice and in hier retinas. It was there the lost mix of love and fanaticism in them. "... Unique vivid red face and crest. Pearly white caruncles sparkled in the sun's rays. The delicate iridescent gray with blue color of its legs. Their song was like that of sirens to pirates."

Silence...

Irene had been silent for a moment, her gaze lost in her memories. Gaping, drool dripped thinly down the side of her mouth, which was curved into a flattened, smiling U-shape. Oswald looked at her strangely. Her mother had frozen as if admiring a painting in a gallery, except that she was doing soin her memory.

"And what happened then?" he interrupted her.

Irene shook her head.

"What?"

"And what happened then?" he reiterated. "The rooster..."

"Your father!" She quickly corrected, frowning. "More fucking respect!"

"Okay!" He shook his head absolutely fed up with all this, curling his tongue up inside his mouth, trying not to let go of his annoyance; it was like wrapping it around her. He amended, "Dad stood in front of you ... and ...? What else?"

"Oh yeah! He stopped in front of me, in the middle of the circle of hens that surrounded me: they had me absolutely cornered and their *cocorocó* was heard every time louder, more intense, more penetrating, but above all more guttural than ever to the point of making me deaf, to such an extent of hearing only them, that sound they were emitting...", her tone of voice had once again turned into something terrifying.

>> Dad, as I said right, stood in the middle of the circle, in front of me. He looked at me powerfully and began to sing. The hens around them began to flap and kick up dust and feathers. So much so that I stopped seeing them. They had built a kind of whirlwind. And only Dad and I were left in the middle of the circle, in the middle of the eye of that whirlwind of dust and feathers.

>> The singing became more and more intense and beautiful. Very beautiful, to tell the truth. I was enchanted, bewitched, bewitched by him: whatever you want to call him. It penetrated my ears roundly, no doubt, like stings in the skin"she said with some torture but pleasure at the same time "like knives in the flesh..." She paused where Oswald waited expectantly. And his voice returned to erotic: "Like a penis enters..."

"MOTHER!" Oswald got up from his seat immediately and started to walk in circles around the room. He didn't want to imagine his mother having sex. And less with an animal! While Irene hadn't told him that she had had sex, and was simply talking about how the music coming from the rooster's throat was getting into her ears, Oswald's mind was thrown to a completely different direction. And even more so when he perceived how her face was changing as well as her voice: orgasmic wrinkles were appearing on it!

"WHAT?!" Irene jumped. "WHAT'S WRONG WITH IT?! YOU ARE AN ADULT, OSWALD!"

He looked at her with his hands anchored at his waist and biting his lower lip. After all, his mother was right: he was an adult; and she hadn't said anything bad. His mind was playing against him, especially when he wanted to wake up from this tremendous nightmare he was living.

He met his gaze at a lost angle on the ground. He remained thoughtful for a moment. Immediately he returned it to his mother, walked towards her, sat down in the chair again and, resting his elbows on the bed, dropped his face into his hands -already dejected- and asked her to continue.

"The singing became intense. I don't know what happened next. I went into a kind of trance, I no longer had control over my body. After that, I don't remember anything else. My vision blurred and I disconnected from the world. I suddenly woke up. I was covered in feathers and dust in the middle of the chicken coop. I didn't know what time or what day it was. Nothing more. I was standing up with difficulty, since I noticed a strong pain in my ovaries that I had never felt before. Around, the hens acted normally, as if nothing had happened. Even your father, he was one more of the chicken coop.

>> I left there feeling strange. Every two steps, I looked back to see what the hens were doing. However, nothing. They were acting normal. I began to believe then that it had been all the product of my imagination and that I had simply passed out due to severe pain in my ovaries, since that same night *Andrés* came to my house for the first time."

"Andrés?" he asked in amazement, turning his head to look at her.

"Yes, Andrés. The one who comes once a month. *El que viene una vez al mes*. The Spanish rhythmical phrase for the women's period, you know."

Oswald nodded, clarifying that he understood what she meant.

Irene continued:

"Until that moment, I had suspected that it had all been a dream: that I had gone to the chicken coop, that my blood pressure had suddenly dropped and I had fainted, that I had dreamed everything I have told you so far, and that I had woken up after an hour and a half or two after regaining consciousness. And I realized that it had not been long time since my mother, when I got home, was finishing putting the silverware for lunch. Your grandparents hadn't noticed that I had passed out or that I was *missing*, let's say. They thought I was playing around there, circling the farm, around the chicken coop. And that he had just happened to be back for lunch as my stomach roar told me that I had to go back for some energy!

>> The rest of the day was normal. Every now and then some strong pain in my belly, but nothing more. It was leaving. It was coming back. It was leaving. It was coming. Thus, irregularly throughout the day. After dinner, I went to bed and fell asleep. I got up at dawn, I don't remember if it was 2, 3 or 4 o'clock. I just remember that the pain was very strong in my belly. It made me want to vomit." She gestured on his face as if he had tasted sour milk, out of date; so exponential was her memory, that Irene felt that her tongue was living it here and now. "I squirmed in bed like a snake whose head has just been cut off. I felt inside me how a small pingpong ball running down my cervix; and suddenly, PLOP!" Irene spread her hands in the air and opened them as if dropping something from them. Her pupils were pointing in the direction of nowhere, her gaze was on her memories and she had begun to accompany her story with movements of her body as if she were reliving the situation at that moment.

She continued:

"I had laid an egg... and I cackled and covered my mouth quickly" she covered her mouth "thinking they would listen to me! But no one listened to me" she took her hands from her mouth slowly and looked at Oswald "Your grandparents were in their tenth dream, more or less."

Oswald nodded his head shyly. I listened to her attentively.

"I sat on the bed," she barely got up from the bed, "and took the egg." She placed her hands in the form of a tray at the level of her chest; she observed the concavity she formed with them. "I looked at it..." she made a categorical pause where she remained gaping and not breathing. After ten seconds, she took a deep breath through her nose and blurted out, "And I didn't know WHAT to do."

>> I looked to the side and saw my nightstand drawer. I kept the egg there. I decided not to tell anyone. I got out of bed and walked to my parents' room. I called my mother by the shoulder and told her that *Andrés* had arrived; I didn't tell her what kind of surprise it had brought me though!" she clarified quickly, firmly raising one of her index fingers and looking at her son. "That was a secret that I kept for myself... forever. They never knew. Nobody knew... until today, that you know.

Oswald took her hands again. He did it lovingly, so that her mother could feel his support. He stroked them gently. She smiled back at him. Oswald said nothing, just allowed her to continue narrating. Irene sighed heavily and continued:

"The problem did not end there. The next day I laid another egg. And the next day, another. The next, another. The next of the next, another. And soon and so on and so on."

>> Regardless of *Andrés*, every day of my life I laid an egg.

"That is to say that the hens had made you a kind of curse?" Oswald asked seriously, though somewhat confused.

"Yes. I guess so. Remember that I told you that I always took their eggs. It was revenge, clearly."

"Like Ricardo's canaries, The Baker?"

"Ricardo lays eggs?!" exclaimed the woman in admiration. She felt her eyes melt into one, like a Cyclops, opening them so wide.

Oswald clutched his head with an exhausted sigh.

"Since when?! I've never known that part of the story!"

Oswald shook his head silently.

"I don't even want to think where those eggs come from!"

"I'm not talking about the eggs, Mom..." he interrupted her reluctantly, dropping the hand that was holding his head heavily. "I mean this being cursed by a group of birds. As he did not allow the canaries to sing, they took his voice from him. As you did not allow the hens to have their eggs, they have made you have them."

"Well..."she was silent, thinking with her hand on her chin, "I think..."she continued thinking; and she concluded quickly: "I think that Ricardo, The Baker is an absolute lie: he has never sung well and has made up that excuse."

"Come on, mom! Please! You can't say this after the hens cursed you! Do you think then that I should believe yours but not Ricardo's?!"

"Mine is more authentic and exotic, Oswald." She looked at him seriously. And you are living it with your wife! Otherwise, tell me about Lily! Anyone can say that he sings badly because of some birds! Come on!!"

"Why have you never said anything, then? Why have you always lied to me about dad?"

"I have never said anything because they would treat me like Ricardo, the baker, what do you think? Do you think that's not enough?" Irene shook her hands in all directions. "No way! The crazy woman with the eggs! It would be the main number of a circus of extravagances! Besides, I've never lied to you. I have *e-di-ted...*" she clarified syllable by syllable "... a truth."

"So Gustavo is the one who raised me ..."

"He's the one who has *HELP me* to raise you," she quickly corrected him with a somewhat murderous look, she didn't like being taken away from the main role. Her right index finger firmly in the air also helped correct Oswald's opinion. "It was when you were about a year old. I tried to get myself a man with the same name who had the rooster that put a spell on me..."

Oswald chuckled, realizing that his mother had been so far-fetched to *edit* the truth to the point of finding a man with the same name as the fowl. He already wanted to see where his mother would take this tremendous fable that was being invented. Although... to tell the truth... He had already doubted that it was such a fabulous fable, but rather he longed to know how far, to what extent of exaggeration, Irene would take such a story.

- I met him after you dropped your beak.

Oswald stared at her in puzzlement. *Beak? Did you say the beak?,* he thought twice. He blinked multiple times at different speeds. He looked to the side. To the other side. He touched his nose. Mouth. Then he grabbed it with his fingers like pliers. *Beak?* he mused again until he let it out aloud:

"Did my beak drop off?"

"Yes,"she answered casually."

Oswald suddenly laughed out of nerves. He got up from his seat and began to walk around the room, touching his mouth and repeating over and over again in a whisper, between question marks, exclamation marks, of both together, or also without either of them: *the beak.*

"I mean…" he said when he stopped in a moment. He looked at his mother and pointed to himself with his hands "… that I was born from an egg?"

"Yes,"she agreed with absolute assurance. "Where else do you think you were born?" before Oswald tried to open his mouth, she went ahead of him and explained with a shrug: "If it was the only way I could have children: through eggs."

Oswald turned around holding his hair. He made a good scramble with them on top of his head. Any bird, hen, canary or whatever, could easily make a nest of it.

Irene asked him to calm down, however Oswald chuckled at the request. He walked to the door and stood in front of it. He peered through the glass into the hallway. He observed people passing by and others sitting waiting to be attended, either to receive some news from a family member or to be seen by a specialist. Then he wondered what would happen if right now he went out and asked each of the people who were there -doctors, receptionists, assistants, students, practitioners, patients, whoever it was-: *Who or what came first: the chicken or the egg?* And after just lingering for a moment broodingly with his arms crossed, he turned his head and look at his mother over his right shoulder. He waited about three, four seconds in a thoroughly silent. Nodding subtly, he turned his eyes back to the hallway.

Oswald understood that if right now, he was sitting there, where that fat lady in a checkered dress was sitting, and somebody would approach her and asked *her what came first?* she would undoubtedly answer that his mother and his wife had come first: two hens not hatched from eggs. Something of which he was not only a witness, but a protagonist.

Oswald heard his mother ask him while he was immersed in his thinking. He turned, sighed deeply as he walked to the bed. He had not understood what Irene had told him earlier, so he asked her to repeat it. She simply asked him what was wrong with him and he replied with a shrug and raised eyebrows.
"I don't know…" he added after dropping his shoulders.
"Would you like to know more?"
"I would like to know how..." he searched his mind "... how it is possible that Lily..." he made gestures with his hands as if trying to catch something ethereal in the air, as if a tiny cotton bud slipped through his fingers.
"Turned into a hen?" –Irene tried to finish the sentence for him.
Oswald nodded.
"Well, I don't know." Irene shook her head. "I thought the curse was over with my menopause. But apparently it's in you and made you passing it on to Lily."
"But how is it possible that you are fine... that you remain a normal person? Lily is slowly turning into a chicken!" He exclaimed truly worried.
Irene noticed it with some distress and patted his head gently.
"I don't know, son. It worries me too. Now I remember well why I passed out! It was not for seeing an egg coming from your wife, but..." she paused and took the opportunity to unexpectedly change her voice to a detective tone, scrutinizing after directing her pupils towards the lower right corner of her eyes, her chin to the right shoulder and concluding Sherlock Holmes: "for having assimilated that the curse had not ended at the time!" Then she looked at him, though without moving her head. "Although I don't understand why Lily is turning into a hen!"

"At first I thought it was something psychotic, but this morning, before you arrived, I saw the dewclaws! Yesterday I touched her hand and her skin was no longer her skin: it was absolutely goose bumps!"

"*Mamma mia!*" she said, pressing her face with both hands like bread on a sandwich.

"I don't know what to do, Mom…" he said, crestfallen, without much encouragement, and sat down next to her again.

Irene leaned forward and gently lifted his face, cupping his chin. She sighed deeply and smiled tenderly. As her mouth drew a flattened *U-shape*, like that, tiny, she stroked the left side of her cheek, marking tiny circles with the pad of her thumb on it. He looked at her. And she looked at him. She contemplated him in the depths of his eyes, entering them as if through a funnel that led her into the soul of her son. She lowered her hand and placed it on his chest. Through the sensitivity of the digital grooves, she heard his heartbeats.

"Whatever it feels in here, Oswald," she said, tapping her index finger just below his clavicle.

Oswald took a deep breath and heard himself inflate and deflate his rib cage. He was aware in such a moment of total sensitivity as his diaphragm expanded and contracted in coordination with his intercostal muscles.

"As I did with you once."

Oswald blinked as if his eyes were tired. It was difficult for him to raise his eyelids, he felt plumb bobs hanging from them. However, it was not because he was sad, but because he sensed the force of his mother's words projected further by the finger tapping against his chest and her cautious gaze penetrating intensely through hers to his being.

"One day I decided to be a mother," Irene continued with decisive and blunt impetus, concentration and, essentially, sincerity. "One day I felt that an egg was special to me, much more than others. One day I felt that *this* egg was the one. That day I felt an unmistakable connection between *that* egg and my soul. That day I began to warm *that* egg with coats, a lamp and caresses and affection. *That* egg, twenty-one days later, hatched.

>> I remember the sound of the shell being beaked and beginning to crack until it breaks. And then... you showed up with your legs, beak and chicken head" at that moment, Irene began to remember the bizarre and disgusting monstrosity that had hatched from that egg and her loving and enchanted tone of voice was on the decline, turning with overtones of disgust; so too, she took her hand out of Oswald's chest and placed her back against the pillow again "... and human arms and trunk..." She tried to hide that saturation in her voice as much as she could, however, it didn't last too long, so She ended up expectorating with filth: "Hey! You were horrible! But I still loved you and I gave you love!" And just as if nothing, she proudly puffed out her chest and changed her voice again: "And look what you've become! A grown man with a huge heart!" She pointed him up and down with both hands.

"How is it that I was born *like* this," Oswald asked, pointing to his mother, not because of her, but because of what she had said about his physical appearance as a baby, "and I ended up *like this*?" He pointed to himself.

Irene giggled through her teeth, it was like an involuntary gasp of pride. She briefly explained:

"As the days went by, both your legs and your head were mutating, becoming more human month by month. It was something like... a monstrous evolution" She made a nasty gesture with her face. She continued with a smile: "You were turning into a real human baby, who was able to walk, of course!, from his birth. I remember you running between my legs the first day, following me everywhere. I know you don't do it much now, you prefer meat, even though you used to love grains. Instead of screaming, you chirped and snuggle up during the night next to me.

>> Over the months, your size increased in a voluminous and accelerated way, asit did the build of your head and legs, which later became legs. At six months, the only thing that remained of that chick was a beak and its diet based on grains, with the occasional invertebrate added; your height, even, was already at the average height of a child of six months. You were walking, obviously, but you couldn't manipulate objects. Ah! You didn't have a nose either! Unquestionably your nostrils lay attached to the top of the beak".

>> During the course of the seventh month, those little holes slid up and back" she touched the bridge of her son´s nose with her left thumb and forefinger"and an upturned shape appeared above it". She delicately pinched the tip of his nose. "By the seventh month, you already had your little *nose*. During the eighth month, your lips were forming behind the beak" she slid her fingers from the tip of his nose to his mouth "until one day, if I remember correctly, it was a week after you were eight months old, it completely detached. Then you started claiming for milk. And everything continued normally and ordinarily, as if you were a child..." she was left wondering what adjective could fit. She stroked her chin with her right hand "... mmm" she continued thinking "... normal, let's say..." She concluded; although she immediately reiterated, waving her hands as a warning sign: "With the exclusivity that you could walk at your six months".

Oswald pondered silently. He had his eyes resting on his mother's gaze, yet he was not looking at her, he was observing himself. It felt... weird! There was a feeling inside him that he didn't know how to describe. It was like a spiral, something that went round and round and round. It was like the symbol of the *Yin* and *Yang* rotating on its axis and drawing circles inside. A mysterious energy ran through his body and forced him to feel uncomfortable and comfortable at the same time; at moments lasting a blink, in absolute peace and for moments of the same quality and harmony, in a cyclopean and phenomenal chaos. It was a distorted, ambiguous truth. An element that was dissociated in its two poles: a truth with its benevolent and malevolent edges! Or rather, a truth, full stop. With all that it entails in its process. That! That was what Oswald was living! A process of absorption, a process of incorporating a truth to a whole load to his transversal and vertical history.

Those were the real poles of truth that were dismantling it, shuffling it and trying to re-amalgamate it, unite it! It wasn't black or white, although it felt that way. It was a truth with all its roots detached and trying to settle into the ground again after being transplanted. Because that had happened, his mother had taken a real slice off and passed it on to him. Now Oswald had to transplant it, and for that he had to remove the soil a little.

"And s-so..." he stammered. "Will the same thing happen with Omelette?" he asked curiously.

"I don't know, son…" She stroked his cheek. "That I don't know".

The Doctors had warned him that his mother would spend the night in the hospital simply for control purposes. As they saw her well, it was highly probable that the next morning she would be able to go home alone. There was no reason for Oswald to pick her up, however, he would call the hospital in the morning and ask to speak with her to see what decision Irene had made: whether to go alone or to be picked up. Knowing his mother, proud about herself from head to toe, without leaving a single homogenized cell in that pride, he supposed that she would decide to walk away; the hospital was not far from home at all.

Returning home in his red F100, he drove home from the hospital. His head went in all directions, angles, directives, parallel and perpendicular that came and went… squares that became cubes, circles, spheres, triangles, pyramids, infinite equations that in a blink of an eye were transmuted into creepy and laughable degree inequalities... there was no way to understand and assimilate everything that was happening to him. It was as if his head was flying in fever, even though he felt wonderful. He was hallucinating, clearly, not being able to logically figure out how his life had taken an unexpected turn and who knows what I know how many degrees beyond 720.

Suddenly, in front of a red traffic light that made him stop the vehicle, he was also forced to stop his thinking and return to reality. In the corner opposite him on his right, was Ricardo's bakery. Its owner, outside smoking a cigarette looking at the sky with one of his hands in the pocket of his white apron. Oswald considered stopping for a moment and making him company. He had no idea how to break the ice if he approached to talk, nor what topic of conversation to bring up.

The traffic light turned green and the Volkswagen in front of Oswald started up. The red F100 followed behind. As he crossed the street and had the bakery by his side, he cast a quick glance to his right through the window and caught the baker's gaze fully focused on the sky as he expelled smoke from his lips with rancor.

Then he saw himself in Ricardo's place and immediately decided that this was not what he wanted for his life, so he did not stop and continued behind the Volkswagen on the way home, thoughtful...

He arrived and found his wife in the park scratching the ground with her feet and looking for worms, insects, grains... he didn't know what, but there she was... When Lily saw him, she cackled with joy and ran to give him a hug and a kiss. At least that still hadn't changed, however, the day would come and he would really miss it. Omellete and Miracle were in the bedroom under a light that warmed them. He stared at them from the threshold. Silently. With a soft yet frank smile.

From the kitchen, Lily asked Oswald if he was hungry and, honestly, he hadn't even eaten breakfast and it was already almost five in the afternoon: his stomach answered for him.

"I understand that's a yes," Lily laughed at the roar. Then she asked, "How was your mother?"

"Good. It's already better. It was an emotional shock", he said approaching the table and pushing one of the chairs aside to sit. "Tomorrow she will go home. She will spend the night in the hospital as they want to control her".

Lily nodded her head and replied softly:

"I understand..." and she handed him a spoon and a plate with a stew of chickpeas, lentils, beans... legumes everywhere, she had nothing else. She sat down in front of him.

Oswald began to eat. He added nothing more.

"And you?" Lily asked. "How are you?"

Oswald took a deep, very, very deep breath through his nose. He bit his lip and put down the spoon without taking his eyes off the plate. Then he looked up and saw Lily in front of him, who was watching him with incredible temperance and mercy. He did not know then what to say to her. He understood through the look that she REALLY needed to know how he felt. Still, he was afraid of hurting her, or angering her, or whatever. He didn't know what words to use to describe what he was carrying inside him.

Lily held out her hand, palm up. Oswald took another deep breath and, immediately after grasping her hand, he released the air from his lungs. A chill invaded his body as he noticed how fast the feathers had advanced on her. The day before, they were not like that.

However, he tried not to give credit to it and, after wrapping her hand with altruism, he replied:

"To tell the truth... a little shocked. These days have been a little... a little... fast", it occurred to him to say. "Both Omelette and Miracle have come to our lives super early and I have a hard time assimilating it."

Meanwhile, Lily was nodding shyly with her upper limb.

"It's hard for me to assimilate being a father. Our lives have changed in the blink of an eye."

"I know, honey. I know... But I also trust that we will be good parents."

"I hope so my love. I hope so..."

Lily leaned her trunk across the table and brought her mouth as close as she could, inviting him to kiss her. He stepped forward and kissed her softly.

"I'll go to brood the children for a while, will you come later?" she said as she walked away.

That phrase had made Oswald fall back to reality, making all that kind of dream acquired in consequence of Lily's sensitivity after his arrival from the hospital, disappear, as well as the elbow of a left-handed child in his first years at school dares to erase what he has just been written, dragging the letters on the page. Also, it led him to think about what Lily saw in him right now, basically *how* she saw him, did she see him as a rooster? and also how she saw herself! Did she understand that she was turning into a chicken? Had she realized it? Had she internalized it? Was she pretending not to be worried about it, not caring at all as long as she was going to be a mother...? Oswald watched her walking away, brooding and brooding. A lot of questions crossed his mind, such as, *don't you feel the changes in your body? The feathers, the spurs, the skin?* Then Oswald touched his mouth with his right index and middle fingers and, after verifying that he had noticed something strange the two times she had kissed his lips, he murmured:

"Does she know she's getting a beak?"

The next day Oswald got up again by the song of Lily, who seemed to have started a kind of competition with the birds singing outside and it was almost impossible to silence her.

He left the sofa and, sleepy, went to the bathroom and took a shower so he could wake up. He dressed in his robe and, in front of the mirror, brushed his teeth. He remembered that he would have to call the hospital to make sure his mother had had a good night and if she wanted him to come and pick her up. However, it was still very early; He would call between 8 and 8.30.

Returning to the sofa, he went to the bedroom door -Lily had closed it before going to sleep the night before- and opened it to ask what she would want for breakfast. However, he could not utter a miserable word. His eyes opened as large as the moons of Uranus and his lower jaw separated from the upper jaw leaving a space where any quail would use as a nest.

A whole night had been enough for Lily's body to make a resounding change: the feathers had grown all over her body -absorbing the wedding dress she was wearing- and her hands, arms, legs and feet had ceased to be human, becoming legs and wings. Her body had shrunk in size, though not by much -she was barely shorter-. Her head was the same, but something of her chin had already started to grow, as if hanging off her, and the glove had been taken by her skin, already forming part of her body. She still didn't have a beak but it was about to bloom, and Oswald no doubt supposed that if it didn't develop that day, it would happen the next day when she woke up; her nose had flattened a bit.

"Good morning, my life!" Lily exclaimed with beautiful joy, flapping slightly with her wings, cuddling her eggs, brooding them like a good mother.

Oswald's astonishment was such that he did not understand what he said.

"Will you make breakfast?"

Oswald only blinked. As he did it twice, Lily understood that his answer had been a *yes*.

"Will you bring it to bed for me, then?"

"What?!" Oswald shook his head. "Excuse me".

"Will you bring me the breakfast to bed?"

"Y... y... yes," the boy replied weakly and turned around. He closed the door behind him and walked to the bathroom as stupid as a zombie; he had felt some of his saliva dripping from his giddy half-open mouth. He had decided that before making breakfast, he would need a new shower. The first had not fully awakened him, NOTORIOUSLY.

When he got out of the second shower, he turned to look in the mirror... In the midst of the absolute silence and calm, he heard the victorious cackle of his wife in the distance, although intense: it was not necessary to go to see if she had laid another egg, he already knew that cackle. Therefore, he returned his eyes to the mirror. Then he faced them to the shower. There would be a third one: he needed to wake up. This time, with REALLY AND INSANELY cold water.

Lily's metamorphosis during the days that followed was insanely accelerated by who knows what cosmic conglomeration. It was just a full moon week, however Oswald didn't know if that had any influence or not. After all, into the following 7 days Lily had completely turned into a hen. That week had been quite chaotic for Oswald, as Lily was still Lily but daubed in feathers: Lily wanted to go shopping, Lily wanted to clean, Lily wanted to cook, Lily wanted to do *this*, Lily wanted to do *that*, Lily wanted to do normal things of Lily without being the Lily *she* used to bein her Lilydays. *Was it Lilyunderstood*? Once Lily was a hundred percent chicken, everything calmed down. However, Oswald had to fight and argue over and over again that first week, warning her that she couldn't go out and shop no matter how much she wanted. To tell the truth, one day she escaped but her husband managed to catch her just in time, since she had gotten on the F100 and, *of course!* she had not been able to start it since she had no fingers to hold the keys and make it start. As a result, and taken by a sense of outrage and helplessness, she had begun to spread a supernatural cackle filled with rage; so it was that Oswald rushed out to grab her and carry her back into the house.

This type of angry screaming had become a habit in every situation that Lily could not handle: like picking up a knife or a broom, or trying to talk to her husband, since she had reached a point where he did not understand her because she only cackled in different tones. The vocal cords had also undergone their corresponding transformation and, day after day, they were losing human pronunciation. It was likely that Lily thought like human and she understood herself, as well as she could hear and understand others. However, when speaking, others heard cackles in different rhythms, while she heard herself speaking normally. And this drove her crazy!

Blasphemies are blasphemies in any field, race, religion, color or whatever. You don't have to understand a language to interpret the essence of profanity: its intonation, rhythm, and punch on hard consonants. Lily's screams had aroused the curiosity of the neighborhood that week and it was not necessary to speak the poultry language, in its gallinaceous branch, to understand it was an angry hen that made those kinds of noises: they were gallinaceous blasphemies, no doubts!

During that week, Oswald was able to notice the increased mass of people in front of his house. His neighbors kept trying to look inside and guess what was going on there. He also noticed that there were people even using binoculars from the adjoining houses, trying to attend to the smallest details of their coexistence with Lily, and the hen, of course! Old Betty even called for eggs.

However, after a week, Lily became a hen absolutely dedicated to her eggs and did not scream anymore. Although she had already been brooding them and with each passing day she dedicated more and more time to them, from the eighth day she hardly got up. There were three in total. She had not laid more than three eggs. However, Oswald doubted that they were all going to be born, since only one of them could have been fertilized: Omelette. After Omelette's birth – in egg form-, they hadn't had sex with Lily again, *unless*... Oswald's sperm had caught up with other eggs and were later delivered by Lily. Anyway, they had to wait the twenty-one days with Lily broody to confirm it.

In the days that followed that first week, Irene went to visit and help Oswald with the cleaning of the house and to support him morally. Oswald could also go to work while Irene stayed with Lily and the eggs at home and everything seemed to return to... normality? *Hell, yes!* At least, it was what it was... The neighbors had also stopped bothering, the only one who kept insisting was Betty.

By the 21st day, Oswald had fully adjusted to his new routine. He would get up, go into the bedroom and greet Lily with a kiss on the little crestor or her beak and go to bathe. Then he would make breakfast for himself and his mother, who would soon be coming to stay with his wife for the day, and Lily would get a special mixture of grains in the room. When he returned from work in the afternoon, he would greet his wife again on the beak or on the crest, share a tea or coffee with his mother, then have dinner, watch some television or listen to the radio and, before going to sleep, he returned to say greet Lily.

Despite the fact that Lily had ceased to be the Lily she had once been, Oswald noticed that some of his old Lily was left in the current Lily. It was as if Lily had truly understood the transformation she had undergone and her neurotic bipolar behavior had finally ceased. Her cells, which had been mired in a chaotic secretion of hormones for the first week of mutation, providing Lily with a tangled identity of duality, now lay coordinated, without battling each other. They were still two Lilys in one: the hen and the human, although currently in synchrony and harmony. The human finally understood that physically she was a hen; the hen discerned that she had her human soul. Because with every kiss that Oswald gave her, she cuddled and shook timidly and lovingly, or stretched her head towards her husband's mouth, so that he could kiss her. And that Oswald had noticed, since when he looked into her eyes, she returned the same affectionate look that she had previously had to all that change that had occurred over her. All the *Lilythings* that *Lilymade* in her *Lilydays* would also transmute: new *Lilydays* would be accompanied by new *Lilythings* and *Lilycustoms*. However, what really mattered was that Lily was still there. And that made Oswald very happy, since he had understood that he would not lose her.

Irene rang the bell as soon as Oswald finished setting the tea on the breakfast table. He had made some toast, left the marmalade and cheese spread, some short bread biscuits, and a few slices of lemon cake his mother had baked the day before.

"Good morning!" The woman greeted when entering the house, hugged her son and kissed him on the cheek, crushing his painted lips on it. Oswald had made a copy of the keys for her just in case something happened during the day when he was away from home and his mother was alone with Lily, so it hadn't been necessary to go and open the front door for her.

"Hi, ma" He greeted her with a hug and a kiss in return. But when he pulled away from her, he wiped her lipstick off his face.

"Why are you taking my kiss off?" She complained as she sat down at the table.

"I'm not taking your kiss off, Mom," he sighed uncomfortably as he walked to the table, he continued to scrub his cheekbone with more and more intensity, since the flamingo pink color that she had stamped seemed to have stuck to his skin like an elephant's foot in the mud. He sat. "I'm taking this paint off, not your kisses", he repeated. "OH MY GOD!" he growled when he realized that his fingers were also smeared with that pink. "Why are you using these cheap brands, mom?!" He got up from his seat and went to a mirror near him.

"I don't have that much money to buy other brands".

"PLEASE!" Oswald protested after noticing in the mirror how the pink had been distributed all over his right side: half of his face was white and the other half was flamingo pink. Then he turned to his mother while pointing a finger at the colored part of his face: "Look at this, Mom!"

Irene shook her head and rolled her eyes up, exhausted. Did not answer.

"You tell me and I'll buy them for you." He returned and sat down with her.

Unexpectedly, Lily screamed. Oswald had not finished leaning his butt on the chair, he jumped up and hit his knee against the edge of the table. Irene was also startled shaking her head and making a sharp movement with her hand and throwing away a piece of cake that she had just caught and was bringing to her mouth.

Mother and son exchanged glances for a few seconds where they remained dumbfounded and then they shot off in unison towards the bedroom converted into a chicken coop.

Lily lifted her head and craned her neck as the double-leaf door swung wide open. She saw her husband and mother-in-law standing under the threshold and watching her expectantly. She managed to notice in their eyes the incomparable brilliance of the illusion; they gleamed the same brilliance of a pearl bouncing a ray of sunlight. Then she knew it was time to raise the right wing...

Oswald and Irene watched as Lily slowly raised her wing and through the space between the wing and her body, a soft and delicate beeping escaped and settled in their ears, slipping like worms in them.

Irene, with her fingers intertwined at the height of her chest and with silent tears escaping and running down her cheeks like hot wax on a cold body, looked at her son: he was smiling open-mouthed and his gaze expressed nothing but happiness. She placed her hand on his back, at the level of his lumbar, and pushed him gently, encouraging him to enter the bedroom and go for that beep that was being seen more and more under the wing.

Oswald stepped forward and Lily cackled contently, her wing nudging gracefully and sweetly at...

"Omelette," Oswald muttered under his breath and studied him carefully.

Omelette was an ordinary chick. He had no human resemblance. His appearance was unquestionably that of a *singing Berger*. And hearing him chirp more attentively made Oswald reproduce in his mind the image of his father...

And then Omelette chirped more vehemently again and made all Oswald's cells twitch and Oswald felt a chill, goose bumps...

And then Omelette chirped again with greater, greater vehemence, penetrating crudely beyond the cells, inserting itself into them like syringes, and reaching the genetic configuration...

And then Omelette chirped again with greater, greater, greater vehemence that Oswald's body suffered a shock as crucial as it was ghostly and hallucinatory that... that... that...

Oswald heard his mother crying out in fear and shock at the same time. He turned and saw her falling to the ground passed out for the second time in the month. He ran to help her, lift her up, however when he stretched out his... *WINGS?!* Oswald exclaimed in amazement, *WHAT, HOW, WHEN?!* he wondered over and over again, confused. He turned to see Lily next to Omelette, who were looking at him from the top of the bed.

"Hi, love!" he heard Lily say clearly. She was not cackling.

"Hello Daddy!" He heard Omelette's fine childish chime. Nor did he chirp.

He had heard them both clearly. *Is it because...?*, he asked to himself, observing his wings for the second time...

Without saying a word, somewhat disoriented, he approached the nearest mirror and contemplated himself: the chirping of his son had made him blink into a *Bergischer Kräher*, that is, into a *singing Berger*.

Omelette had given him back his identity.

Trouble Dying

•

Part 1

After all, it was like the myth said: the light at the end of the tunnel. And there Martha was after opening her eyes. A long tunnel with an incandescent white light at the end. The woman had to cover her face, and shaded her eyes after opening her eyelids because the brightness was dreadful, dreadfully intense.

She looked at herself.She found herself dressed in tight jeans, a fairly baggy plaid shirt and trainers. She wore her glasses with the huge, slightly orange, square frame that reached up to her eyebrows.

His short blond hair was still there, dyed to slightly deflect his true age,with the modern haircut that her hairdresser had been doing for a year now, making such a detour appear to be a new age twist.The whole look had taken a little more than ten years off, so she felt like she was 58 again.

She touched her body, from her ankles to her head.When she ran her hands over her tits, she grabbed them and made them bounce ethereally; she was surprised that they didn't hang down as much as she remembered in her 58s, so she took another 8 years off herself.

And immediately after touching them, she went back to his backside and repeated the same thing. She grabbed both cheeks and bounced them a little bit. *Oops*, she was pleasantly surprised and decided to take off another 5 years. Then she pulled down his trousers a bit and noticed that they were still there…

"You sons of a bitch!" cursed. "Not even death can take them away!"she joked, pulling up her trousers again. "Cellulite!" So, instead of subtracting, she added another 3 years. So, the count gave her about 48 years old. Although saying she had died at 48 wasn't so good, not even feeling 48, so she added back the 25 she had taken off.

"MARTHA!" was suddenly heard.

The woman was startled.

"God?"she exclaimed, looking about in all directions.

There was a sigh of exhaustion, as if the person was tired of hearing the same question repeatedly. Martha noticed that the voice came from an antique brass telephone with a dialling wheel. It was lying to her left, hanging on the wall.

"No, no. I'm just an employee."

Martha made a face like... well, it was not clear what face she was making, she simply wrinkled up her left side, puzzled. *"Employee?"* she wondered to herself.

"Yes, employee, Madam"the boy answered.

But how!, her eyes nearly fell out of their sockets, truly amazed that the man had read her mind.

"Yes, Madam..., we can read your mind. We know everything about you. You are going to Heaven. There is no thought you can hide. There is nothing you can hide from us."

"Are you an angel then?"

"No, I'm not."

The lady was puzzled. Her face was more confused. Was she a demon punished to work in Heaven?

"I am a theology student, and I am doing my internship."

Martha went blank in her mind. She looked to the side, towards what seemed like the end of the tunnel, and then returned her gaze to the phone.

"Theology student?" she asked curiously; and then she asked directly, without hesitation, anyway if she had thought the question through, she would have read out to him.

"Are you dead?"

"No, no. I'm telling you I'm a theology student, Madam."

"So, are you alive?"

"Yes, I'm alive."

"On Earth?"

"Yes," he answered with a weary sigh.
"I mean, alive, alive!"
"Yes, Madam"
"But how?"
"The Vatican influences Heaven, Madam."
"The Vatican?"
"Tell me what you think the Vatican is for, Madam."

Marta stood there pale and with no response. She didn't know what to answer.

"A lot of people from the Vatican work here" the boy added. "They do all the paperwork and controls for those who die and begin their journey to Heaven."

WHAT?, exclaimed Martha to herself. Her guts contracted. She hadn't been a Catholic person at all in her life; at least, she hadn't been a churchgoer entirely. She had been to the occasional mass. She used to sing a song or two. She knew the *Alleluia*, at least. *Lamb of God* too. She also prayed - when she needed a miracle - the *Our Father*, the *Hail Mary*, and the occasional *Glory Be to the Father*.

Maybe they'd take a test? Maybe they'd make her sing? Why hadn't anyone told her this before? *The Church must report this!*, she complained to herself, and now that she was dead, she was finding out about it! And what kind of paperwork was the boy talking about, by the way? She supposed they should have everything digitised by now, and all they'd make her do was sign a couple of papers and that would be it.

"What do you think the Church is preparing you for, then, Madam?", asked the boy, and added, "Don't complain!"

The boy had read her mind again and did not like that attitude at all. However, she had no other choice. She realised that the Vatican had more control than Instagram and Facebook combined.

"Please, Madam, I must continue with my protocol as I must go and help another newcomer... We have been very busy lately, please excuse me," he requested politely. He continued: "Please, ahead you will find an electronic conveyor belt, like the one at the airports, which will take you to the light. You don't have to walk; you will just enjoy the ride. If you want to stop the conveyor belt, you can stop it by using the word *stop*, and you can resume it by using the word *forward*."

"You will see along the tunnel many moments of your life; you will re-live them. Once you reach the end, you will be greeted by a colleague, a kind of bellboy who will take you to the next procedure. By the way, whoever greets you, don't call him *bellboy*, they don't like to be called that way," he laughed low, as if in confidence. "They call themselves the *Golden Ark Receptionists*, although it's a very long name and internally we call them *bellboys*. Thank you very much, enjoy your stay!"

The boy hung up. He hadn't given her room to say a word. "*Enjoy your stay?*" she wondered with a frown, "*I suppose it was ironic, wasn't it?*" she scratched her head doubtfully.

Marta then turned and walked towards the tunnel. It was long. The light could be seen distantly, but it was dazzling nonetheless, not as it had been when she first opened her eyes. Now her pupils had adjusted a little more.

So, she moved forward. A few steps ahead the conveyor belt of which the boy had spoken, began. It was not running, though. She put one foot. Then the other. And the conveyor belt started. She wobbled a little, so she balanced her arms.

Paintings in elegant frames were spread along the tunnel. Each of them projected different moments of her life, using images, photos, paintings themselves, videos, sounds, voices, sensations on the skin, tastes, smells...

Within the frames, everything came to life in such a particular way that it made Martha part of the picture: whole memories, solely captured by her whole being as such, even those in the womb that she would never have remembered.

Each memory and projection embraced her like a hen warming her chicks. To tell the truth, Martha had to be honest and, despite all the criticism against the Church, she had to accept that the Vatican had worked very well in selecting her memories to project her into the tunnel when going to the light. A few tears had fallen from her eyes, and she had to wipe them away with the back of her hand several times, also with the pad of her thumbs.

Suddenly, one of the most beautiful memories is when she was breast-feeding from her mother's breast, while her mother was looking into her eyes with infinite love and singing to her; Marta could feel the vibrations of her mother's chest and the warmth of the milk and its nutrients as if she was living it at that very moment; was interrupted by a group of voices in the background, sounding like an interference on a telephone. Martha burst out with the command Stop! for the conveyor belt to stop.

It was a whisper of several different timbres that Martha could not understand where they were coming from. Her memory had interrupted her projection process, but the voices were still there, annoying her.Suddenly, she noticed that there were some speakers located about three metres above her and she sharpened her hearing towards them: they were her daughters.

Immediately she thought they had died too, but it didn't take much longer than a few seconds to grab her head with both hands, entwined her fingers in her hair and tug lightly at it, saying:

"Not even being dead I can be in peace,"she let her hair down and shook her fists in the air in weariness. "Fed up, fed up!" she dropped her arms to her sides and sighed vehemently. She stayed for a while listening to the conversation.

"Let Theresa have that," said Gabriella. "I'll take her shoes."

"I don't want her old lady's coat! Not even if I washed it with the COVID-19 virus would I get rid of the smell!"

"I think Mum has had the virus for years now: graceless for clothes, please!" laughed Ernestina.

"And for the choice of names either!" said Teodora, pointing her index finger at herself and her older sister Ernestina repeatedly with speed. "I'd rather keep their hot lingerie, one and a thousand times over."

Son of the bitch!, Martha exclaimed to herself. But she quickly realised that she was the mother of those four women: Ernestina, Theodora, Theresa, and Gabriella. She had born them in that order; the first two were two years apart; then between Theodora and Theresa it had been about five years, and then another two for the birth of Gabriella.

"Hot lingerie?" Gabriella asked in surprise. She was the most discreet of the four of them.

"Yes, indeed!" said Ernestina with an air of obviousness and then added: "I've found her..." she fell silent unexpectedly.

There was a pause...

"What?" a voice whispered, and Martha didn't know which of her daughters it was. Their voices were very similar.

A whisper was heard as if inviting the group to come closer.

Fuck! said Martha. She knew her daughters from head to toe, especially the eldest. Ernestina had found it and was about to reveal her secret to the other three... She covered her face with both hands, feeling ashamed.

Soon Ernestina was heard to mutter a little louder than usual as if speaking a secret aloud for only her three sisters to hear:

"I have found it, a *dildo*."

Martha held her forehead as she shook her head as her other three daughters immediately stifled a slightly exaggerated breath of confusion.

"Mummy, what's a dildo?" A little voice said, and the woman held her head tighter. It was Analía, one of her youngest granddaughters.

"Madam, be quiet!" they said suddenly, and Martha was startled, holding the same hand she had on her forehead to her chest.

With her hands behind her back and a smile from ear to ear, a woman had stood beside her; she was about the same age as she was, though several centimetres shorter. Her hair was short, curly, and puffy, like a poodle toy with frizz and static after a bath. She wore oval earrings of precious stones surrounded by gold edges. She had a tiny nose and wore glasses, though not as fashionable as Martha's, but rather round and small.

Her eyes were also small and looked even smaller with long eyelashes. His mouth was thin, though painted red and with a certain pattern above the upper lip to make it appear wider and fuller. Her cheeks had orange freckles and seemed to have more on the right side than on the left, lying well under her eyelids.

She wore a long pastel pink summer skirt with white spots and a loose white T-shirt. She wore leather sandals and walked with a slight stoop. Martha realised that the curvature was not due to the weight of her tits, as the woman hardly had any.

"I used to wear it too" added the lady. "It's normal, indeed! I brought it with me!" she pointed happily and uncovered her hands, which were behind her back. The dildo was swaying in her right hand from side to side in front of the woman's eyes with a (and tempting! Martha had to agree) swaying motion.

Martha didn't know what to answer. Besides, she didn't understand why the woman was there: Was she just another employee or was it the devil who had come to seduce her in some extravagant way with that thick, veiny thing? She simply stared at her for a moment and then asked:

"Sorry, but... What's your name?"

"Hannibal" she answered quickly, shaking her rubber penis and smiling more than usual, which made it clear that they were great buddies; to which she added, putting her other hand next to her mouth as if she were going to tell her a secret: "But I call it *The Clitoris Minstrel.*"

"I didn't want to know so much detail, madam!" she said, grabbing her forehead.

"Old people like you need it more than the world thinks you do" she continued without crediting her.

"What's your name?" Martha insisted.

However, the woman continued to shake the *dildo* back and forth as if it were nothing... Martha had already begun to get annoyed at the way the thing was moving in the air. It was a bit of an uncomfortable situation.

"Blue pill? Please! That's not good enough, woman! The man reaches a point where he needs to be discarded! Bye-bye! Out! Doesn't work! Throw away!"

"Madam!" she stopped by grabbing her shoulders and looking at her with intensity. Immediately, she grabbed the hand with which she was holding the dildo and pulled it down, placing it beside her body. She looked back into his eyes, her own eyes wide open. "What's your name..."

"Ah, me? Rosy"

"Hi Rosy, I'm Martha" she extended her hand.

"Rosy," she said, imitating the gesture. "My name is Rosy."

When she gave her hand to shake it, Martha took the dildo without noticing it, since the woman had extended her right hand, and she admired the thickness: at first sight, it seemed less; and she was also surprised by the protuberances... But she immediately let it go and changed hands.

"Oh, excuse me!" laughed Rosy. "I didn't realise" and she greeted her with a squeeze of her other hand.

"Are you an employee here?"

"An employee? Me? Oh, no! I died ten or fifteen minutes ago, I think!"

Martha looked to one side. Then the other. She wondered if the tunnels were individual. Then she asked her:

"And what are you doing here?" Martha straightened up and shook her shoulders weakly.

"My life is boring, woman..."

"What?" Martha's eyes wanted to pop out of their sockets.

"Yes. I don't want to see my life again. I asked the student from the Vatican if I could change tunnels and he said yes. They opened a little door in the wall for me" she turned around and pointed back with her rubber penis. She turned back to Martha at once. "It's gone now, though. They closed it."

Marta put her hands on her hips. She took an extremely deep breath. If she could have sucked air in through her ears, she would have done it too. She held the air in her chest.

She looked to one side again, to the other, looking for someone responsible for this. Was there a *Customer Service -Customer* with a capital letter by the way- *line*?. She thought of the old phone at the beginning of the tunnel through which the boy had spoken to her. The thing is, she didn't know which number to dial either.

She played with her mouth, biting her lips together discontinuously and diversely. Then she let the air out slowly and began to move her right foot, as she always did when patience had her on the edge of exhaustion: without lifting her heel, she tapped the end of her foot with a certain timidly paused frenzy. It was a way of releasing accumulated tension so that her veins wouldn't burst from so much pressure of accumulated carbon dioxide and without being able to be emancipated. It couldn't be possible... Even in death, she couldn't be in peace. And the worst thing was that at the same time, she could still hear her daughters talking to each other in the background and mocking her or arguing about her possessions.

"Look, Martha...," said Rosy. Although it quickly crossed her mind to ask something different: "I can address you informally, can't I?"

Martha, who was looking to the side, glanced at her twice out of the corner of her eye. She tapped her right foot more lightly. She bit her lips again, and at the third sidelong glance, she nodded her head.

"Look, Martha. I promise not to disturb you," she raised the hand with the rubber penis to her shoulder as a sign of promise.

Martha watched the dildo wobbling back and forth like a banana already turning black.

"Oops, sorry!" Rosy exclaimed and switched hands, showing the palm of her other hand on her shoulder.

Martha let out a chuckle at the woman's unexpected reaction. And she thought that at a certain point, it might be fun and more pleasant to share her memories with someone else. After all, Rosy seemed to be a rather funny and amusing woman; she had a certain touch of madness and humour that Martha rather liked it. And to tell the truth, she didn't have any other choice either...

"All right, let's go!" she announced, and the conveyor belt started to run.

Part 2

Rosy didn't stop talking for a second and talked about absolutely all her memories. All of them. A-L-L. Not only that, but she talked over the projections and did not allow Martha to enjoy them. And it wasn't just that she was talking to her, but from time to time, when Martha asked her to please be silent, Rosy started talking to Hannibal.

Yes, Hannibal. Exactly. Her dildo. She kept talking in hushed tones about the projections of Martha's memories as if Hannibal were answering her, continuing the conversation, as if it were participating in it like a drunk man at the bar with his usual group of strangers.

"Rosy," Marta said, turning around and giving her an intense look and then looking at the dildo. 'Hannibal,' she said, and when she did it, she instantly asked herself if she was really talking to a rubber penis as if it were a person. "Will you please be silent?"

Rosy nodded and made the dildo move as well by way of accepting the woman's invitation to be silent. However, when she turned to continue enjoying the projection in front of her, Rosy started a new conversation with Hannibal. First arguing, as if angrily shutting it up...

"Have you not listened? Shut your mouth, Hannibal!"

And so, it went on, like a children's fight...

"I said shut up! You started it! Shut up!"

Though immediately a giggle...

"Oh, Hannibal! Heh heh heh!"

And then a chuckle of complicity...

"Oh, Hannibal! Not in front of Martha! Ji, ji! Not that, Hannibal!"

And immediately any kind of conversation was connected to the above...

"I think that's one of the daughters," Rosy pointed out while also contemplating one of the memories, "what do you think?"

Martha just took a deep breath and tapped her right foot to release tension. She was holding her forehead, as well as wrinkling her face by rubbing her eyes with her index finger and thumb, while the other fingers did the same with her cheeks. It was also a way of helping with the tapping of the right foot to release tension.

At one point, the projections stopped and so did the conveyor belt. The women staggered at the unexpected circumstance and exchanged glances between them.

"What did you play?" Martha accused Rosy.

"Nothing!" the woman defended herself.

Then they heard a whistling sound coming from up ahead. It was a singing whistle, typical of a labourer working alone. They saw a man standing in front of what looked like a metal box attached to a pole on the side of the tunnel belt. He was dressed like a plumber, he had the classic Mario Bross look, and he even had his moustache, although his shirt was yellow, and he was wearing a tool belt. They approached him.

"Good morning..." greeted Martha.

"Hello, madam, good morning!" He said with great joy.

Martha liked the way the moustache smiled since it was so bushy that it covered both lips almost completely. It was as if the man was talking without opening his mouth, doing ventriloquism. She found it very funny and congenial.

"Good morning!" repeated the man, looking at Rosy and giving her a little bow with his head.

Rosy blushed and simply waved her hand, wiggling her fingers.

"Tell me, ladies... what can I do for you?" he asked with tremendous kindness.

"I'd like to know what happened in my tunnel," she looked around, pointing to the empty projection walls. At that moment, she saw that her colleague was slightly walking sideways and leaning slightly back to keep an eye on the man's backside.

"I think we'll be here for a while, madam. The power station has detected a malfunction in your tunnel that may cause it to open a direct gateway to Hell."

"A direct gateway to Hell?"

"Yes, yes. It happens very occasionally. It's unusual. But, well, unfortunately, you've had it. If I don't fix it, when you get to the end of the tunnel you won't find the buttons, but some other creepy creature."

"Wow," she thought for a few seconds and then added, "Did you say *power station*?"

"Yes, madam," he replied, turning back to the metal box, and continuing to remove the screws to get it open.

"What kind of energy?" she asked curiously as she watched out of the corner of her eye as Rosy stared at the man's buttocks like fresh lemonade on one of the hottest summer days. She noticed that some drool was dripping from his mouth.

"Theocentric, madam."

"And what is *Theocentric Energy*?"

"It comes from people praying and praying. What do you think the Church needs people to pray for?" he chuckled and looked at her quickly out of the corner of his eye. "It's to keep these tunnels running so they don't have to pay for electricity. Do you know how much electricity it would cost to run these things 24/7? PUF! YOU WON'T BELIEVE IT! They need people to be believers to generate energy, no matter how: praying at home, in the temple, going to confession, asking for forgiveness, reading the Bible... Ouch!" complained the man and jumped up and down. "What are you doing madam?" he turned angrily and scolded Rosy as he stroked his backside in a kind of frenzy.

The woman had approached him while he was distracted talking to Martha and had grabbed one of his buttocks with her five fingers like a small child picking up play dough and squeezing it through her fingers.

Rosy responded by shaking her shoulders like a bird after wiping her feathers with her beak, growled at him sensually like a feline as she bit her lower lip and, with the same hand that had hooked one of her buttocks like a blade in the flesh, executed a delicate catlike scratch in the air. Then she raised her other hand and shook Hannibal in the air; she winked at him.

"Won't you be my Adam and I'll be your Eve and we'll put the energy back into this tunnel?"

Martha felt embarrassed. Even more so when the man asked her while pointing at the other with his thumb over his shoulder:

"Who is this nymphomaniac?"

"I don't know her!" Martha immediately pulled herself together, showing the palms of her hands as if a policeman had given her the order to STOP. "She appeared in my tunnel."

"Don't you want to play, Mr. Plumber?" Rosy asked without hesitating.

The man turned to glare at her.

Martha signalled Rosy to shut up over the technician's shoulder.

"No, thank you, madam. And I'm not a plumber," he then turned back to Martha. "I have to ask you to change tunnels, please," he pointed to the side and an opening in the wall magically opened.

Martha walked to the opening.

"And when can I come back?" she turned around.

"At some point... they'll tell you over the loudspeaker."

"At some point?" she repeated puzzled.

"There is no such thing as time here."

Martha sighed exhaustedly through her nose.

"Ah and take your friend with you!" he pointed the screwdriver at her.

"She's not my friend," Martha clarified, this time glaring at him as she grabbed Rosy by the wrist. She didn't want to go with her, she didn't feel like it at all, but if she left the woman with the man, she would screw him over and not allow him to work in peace, so her tunnel would never be repaired and, in the end, she wouldn't be able to go back to it. "Come on, Rosy!"

She growled at him sensually for the last time and followed her colleague.

They left the Mario Bross-looking man behind after crossing the threshold, as the opening closed in the blink of an eye after they set foot in the adjoining tunnel.

They came across a woman apparently the same age as them, who greeted them politely and introduced herself as Naomi. She had a certain oriental feature, at least the crow's feet drooping at the sides of her eyes gave that expression. She was about Rosy's height, though a little more hunched over. She wore thin, oval glasses with a string of tiny pearls behind them. Her voice was a little raspy as if not quite cured of the flu.

Marta apologised to herself and Rosy for having got them into her tunnel and explained that they were repairing hers, that as soon as they had done so, she would return immediately - she had clearly not put Rosy in the sentence: the verb used had been in the first person singular: she would return to HER tunnel.

"What difference does it make! This tunnel is not mine either!" she waved her right hand in the air.

Martha and Rosy looked at each other questioningly. Clearly from the Vatican or from Heaven, they were doing something wrong. Martha didn't know exactly who was responsible for the administration or management of the tunnels to the light, but what she knew for sure was that whoever had won the bidding for the construction, maintenance or concession of the tunnels was using the money for something else entirely, since they had no electricity costs either, or she had just learned that from Mario Bross. *Outrageous...*, she sighed, *Even in Heaven there is corruption*, she shook his head.

"Apparently, it belongs to a certain Prajna, from what I've been seeing," Naomi detailed, holding her hands behind her back. "A Buddhist girl..."

"Buddhist?" the other two jumped in unison.

"Yes, apparently... they got the wrong route and when she died, they put her in a Christian tunnel. I understand she must be in my tunnel because I'm in hers. Do you by any chance know where I can make my claim?"

Rosy denied it with a shake of her head. Martha hesitated for a moment and then replied with a no. She thought to herself that there was no corruption in Heaven. She corrected herself: in religion there was corruption. In any case, she did not stop thinking *outrageous...* with the same hint of disgust and disappointment as she had done before. How was it possible that once dead, no religion could ensure the welfare of such a person?

They played the conveyor belt along the Prajna tunnel and enjoyed the story. As it did not belong to any of the three of them, they watched it as if it were a film at the cinema; the only thing missing was the popcorn. Rosy and Naomi had become close friends. To tell the truth, they both talked a lot and made naughty comments; Naomi was a bit more discreet than Rosy.

Martha, meanwhile, was eye rolling from time to time and trying to find a clock in the tunnel that would tell her how much time had passed, as she wanted to get back to her tunnel. Above all, though, it was a good time to get rid of Rosy and her... Hannibal, who, by the way, had already started to socialise very well with Naomi, too... However, Martha knew she would never see that clock, not even to know when it would be *some time...* as Mario Bross had told her.

Part 3

The *Sometime...* never came. Prajna's life was longer than *Titanic*, the *Harry Potter* and *Lord of the Rings* sagas and all the latest Di Caprio films at once, albeit played at a speed 10 times slower and duller than Martha's own dead life in the Prajna tunnel itself.

The conveyor belt stopped two metres from the light threshold. Nothing was visible on the other side. They crossed it and were greeted by bellboys. Ahead they could see a huge building in the shape of an ark: the *Golden Ark*, as the little boy who was studying theology *or whatever* had indicated to them.

As they went along, Martha could hear the other dead people complaining about the tunnels, about how poorly they were working. Occasionally, the other person could be heard saying something nice. However, they were more complaints than nice things.

Walking through the clouds was a strange but beautiful feeling. It was like walking on a thin layer of snow surrounded by fluffy pearly gardens. At the back of the ark was a large gate with golden bars that stretched nearly seven metres high and ran sideways to infinity. And behind it, an immense garden of deep green with people strolling everywhere.

"Is that Eden?" asked Marta to the bellboy who was accompanying them, pointing with her index finger.

"No, madam. It's a simple garden."

"So, Eden?" said Rosy.

"Eden is part of the garden. It is a private country and only God lives there. As a matter of fact, God, his family and many well-known biologists and biotechnologists."

"And what are they doing there?" Naomi interrupted rather curiously as she didn't understand how religion had become mixed up with science.

"They create new species. They test them and all that sort of thing before they send them to Earth."

"And Darwin is there?" asked Martha, understanding, as did Naomi, that he had questioned the theological theories to such an extent that he had completely overturned them with the theory of evolution after publishing *The Origin of Species*.

"He is the right-hand man."

Naomi and Martha looked at each other and nodded to each other with an air of astonishment. After all, religion and science were one and the same.

"And will we meet celebrities?" Rosy wanted to know eagerly. "I'd like to meet Lady Di."

Madam, Lady Di lives in a private country house outside of Garden 104.

Rosy immediately stood up in shock. She put her hands on her hips and opened her mouth wide in astonishment at what the bellboy had said. Then she picked up her pace again, but with greater agility so that she managed to walk past the bellboy and his companions and stopped them in their tracks, facing the boy with an air of annoyance:

"Isn't it that once we're dead we're all equal?"

"Those are things they make up on Earth, madam. Class is not negotiable," smiled the bellboy, though without showing his teeth. "Excuse me," he added, putting a hand on her shoulder, "we must move on."

"I'm not moving until I get an explanation!" she glared at him, bowing her head slightly. She wanted at that moment to annihilate him by digging her fangs into his jugular and tearing off his flesh.

"*Being* is a condition and we inherit that from the Lord," he explained, "and Lady Di *is* of a certain class to which you do not belong because you *are not* that class, do you understand?"

"Like my name is Rosita Isabel Rodríguez Vargas, no, I don't understand!"

"Well, there it is. There you have it. You said it yourself: *Rodríguez Vargas* is not an aristocratic surname."

"I don't mind three horns!" she shook her head.

"Madam, this is simple. Have you washed dishes?"

"Why do you ask that question?" she waved her hand in the air as if shooing flies away from her face. Clearly, it was with her peculiar toy.

"Have you washed dishes?" insisted the bellboy.

"Yes, and proudly!" she exclaimed, standing up straight, drawing her shoulders back, thrusting her chest forward, lifting her chin and showing her forehead.

"Well, Lady Di didn't. Now, if you'll excuse me," he said and pushed gently to the side to make way for him.

Rosy was SHOCKED, completely dumbfounded, much more so than before, and speechless to continue arguing. She looked at Martha and Naomi for their support in the discussion but they both shrugged their shoulders and held their palms up to the sky, not knowing what to say to her.

"Besides," added the bellboy, turning to gesture with his hand for Rosy to please come with him, "people come to Heaven to seek peace, don't they?" And he turned again to continue walking to the front and explaining to the other two women next to him. "Therefore, celebrities don't want to be constantly disturbed, madam. That's why we try to give them the same conditions of privacy as they had on Earth, or better."

"And how many gardens are there?' asked Naomi. 'Did you say that Lady Di lives in Garden 104?"

Rosy joined the group again.

"There is a single garden divided into a number of districts," explained the bellboy. "And then there's Eden, which is another style of garden, a special one. And yes, you can get to 104 after taking a Moses in Exodus."

"What do you mean by *Moses* and *Exodus*?" Martha looked at him strangely.

"Ah, yes! *Moses* is the means of transport here in Heaven, it's a kind of train. And *Exodus* is the central station. Very good!" he said suddenly, clapping his palms together after a clap and bowing slightly with his upper trunk. "Here I leave you in line. I must go and get some more people. Have a nice day!"

Due to the distraction of the talk, they had not previously noticed how long the line was to enter the ark. Noticing it, they looked at each other and didn't say a word. The people who would have called for a single comeback concert of the Spice Girls and the Backstreet Boys singing together on one stage were less than a quarter of the number of people waiting to enter the holy ship.

They understood that time didn't matter there. 10 hours more or 10 hours less didn't matter! They were already dead. Patience was part of the process of getting into the garden, but this was the last straw! From the front of the queue, the rumour had spread that not all the counters were open and that the service was quite discouraging, because even if they were all open, it wasn't entirely efficient either, as the most novice in the job forgot to ask for documentation and that slowed down the process.

At least that's what they heard them say to those in front of them, who had heard it from those who had, in turn, ahead and so...

"With good reason, they call this the Eternity!" said Naomi after a deep sigh, and Martha responded with a grimace of her mouth and an arching of one of her eyebrows in disgust.

"Documents?" Rosy wondered aloud. "But what documents are they asking for?"

"Well, I don't know, Rosy," Martha shook her head softly. "But nobody has any documents, look," she pointed out how the people were empty-handed, with no papers or briefcases or anything like that. It must be a miscommunication. "Notice that this gossip comes from up ahead,' she raised her arm showing the beginning of the line. 'It starts out as one thing and ends up here as another."

Little by little, the women moved forward in the line. Martha looked back and noticed that the line grew longer and longer. She saw how the bellboys were bringing more and more people. She wondered how many people were dying in the world, and what was happening to non-Christians like Prajna.

Was this where they were diverted to other places? She saw a woman brought by one of the bellboys, arguing with him, telling him that she did not belong to Heaven, that she had to be resurrected. Then she thought it was Prajna - Martha asked her colleagues if they thought so too.

The bellboy told her that she had to wait, that he was not responsible for such a job, that he knew nothing about it; that his job was only to receive people after the light at the end of the tunnel and guide them to the ark line. Then there, the administrative staff would refer them to an HR manager to review their case. However, he, as one of the bellboys, could do nothing about it.

At that moment, a boy dressed in a brown beret, a T-shirt and shorts whiter than clouds, thin black braces, and trainers of a lighter shade than the beret, approached them and made them forget about Prajna.

He handed a flyer to each of them without saying anything and continued to hand them out in the line to the people behind them. The flyer read *Via Crucis Travel*. And then it continued:

Via Crucis Travel
The best option for your eternal holiday!
Great offer for this long weekend!

"Long weekend?" asked Naomi curiously as she re-read the sentence. She didn't take her eyes off the flyer.

"Yes, as far as I remember, I was in hospital around Easter," said Martha, frowning and reading the flyer.

We travel to Hell.
Get to know:
- The Valley of the Fallen Angels.
- The Satan's Cabin.
- The Hades' Vineyard.
- The Grand Canyon of the Abyss.
- The Lake of Fire

Martha was speechless. She raised her head, looked back at the flyer delivery man and again looked back at the flyer to re-read the offer and then concluded:

And don't worry, we'll bring you back!

This was clearly a joking exclamation. And then the contact:

Places are limited.
If you are interested, please book your place at: viacrucis.info@viacrucisviajes.com

"Do they have internet?" said Rosy.

"Apparently..." replied Naomi.

They kept the flyer just in case and chatted about this and more as they waited in the queue. The queue went on and on until at some point they crossed the door and entered the building. It was as cold as entering a church and there was heavenly music playing in the background.

There were seats all over the place, many customer service boxes on the opposite side, stairs here and there, machines with touch screens broadcasting the appointments, and monitors hanging everywhere indicating which number was next and to which box one had to go to be attended at. The walls were lined with Saints' portraits as well as figures.

A central chandelier hung from the ceiling of the ark, displaying such an exquisite, luxurious and exotic arachnid skeleton, with who knows how many incalculable legs it had that it was impossible to take your eyes off it. Bathed in gold, it emanated an exceptional glow, and tiny, delicate crystals in the shape of snowflakes were suspended from its limbs.

The lights, located at the ends of each arm, were the shape and size of giant's tears, albeit inverted.

At the end of the line inside the ark, which did not extend very far, by the way, just before the appointment dispenser, there was a structure about three metres high escorted by two angels dressed as Roman warriors, with swords held in their scabbards at the side of their bodies and bows and arrows like backpacks on their backs between their retracted wings.

The structure looked rather like a metal detector... but *who would come in here with a weapon*, Martha thought strangely; how could a terrorist attack be possible in Heaven?

And at that very moment, a horrifying crackling sound coupled with a frantic flashing of a red light that acted as a warning eye made itself feel as if a man passed through the metal detector! The guardian angels approached him and instructed him to proceed to a door on the other side of the appointment dispenser.

"Do you think he came to Heaven with a knife?" Rosy asked the other two.

Naomi shrugged her shoulders and an *I don't know* face.

"I don't think he could have brought a weapon with him," Martha doubted.

"Maybe it's a gun he inherited from his father and he wanted to bring it with him. Let's see, it's probably discharged!" said Naomi.

"Do you think there are terrorist attacks in Heaven?" Martha spat out the uncertainty that had been on her mind.

"You mean like someone from Hell sneaking in and planting a bomb?" Naomi looked at her from the side, not very convinced-. "Mmm… I don't think so..." she shook her head.

"And what do they have the metal detector for?" Martha pointed it out more doubtfully. She then took out the tourism leaflet and showed it to the others. Someone must have snuck in on one of these trips to the *Via Crucis*. "Don't fuck with me! This is a hoax!" She shook the leaflet in the air "There's something fishy going on here!"

"Do you think so?" Naomi hesitated.

Martha tilted her head and arched her eyebrows as if affirming what she had said earlier. Then she put the leaflet away again.

"Don't take my Hannibal away from me!" Rosy was terrified and hugged her rubber penis to her chest as if it were her teddy bear.

The other two giggled.

In less than two minutes, the three of them found themselves in front of the metal detector waiting for one of the angels to give them the order to cross. Martha was in the first place. Naomi was second and then Rosy followed; she had placed herself last as she wanted to enjoy more time with Hannibal in case it was taken away from her. And there she had it squeezed against her chest.

One of the angels indicated with a slight nod to Martha that she could go forward, and she did so. She crossed the threshold, and the bell began to sound, and the red light began to flash in a blink of an eye. Martha turned over her shoulder to look at her colleagues with wide-eyed surprise, not understanding why the metal detector had reacted. Both Naomi and Rosy returned the same look of misunderstanding, as their minds had also been painted white.

Both angels approached her and held her arms tightly so that she couldn't move; Martha felt like a prisoner in the most dangerous cellblock. One of them approached her ear and advised her to go to the same door through which the other man who had already been buzzed had disappeared, on the other side of the appointment dispensers. He also told her that, once through the door, she should look for number 4, that her number was 4.

His voice was very sensual and husky, booming, like a hairy alpha male with an exaggerated level of testosterone. He had also brushed her cheek delicately with his thick shaved beard, about two millimetres long, and that had made her a little horny in the blink of an eye; she felt her body begin to melt like a bucket of butter near the cooker.

However, the image of Rosy flirting with Mario Bross came to her mind and she identified herself a little. But as she was *NOT* Rosy, and she didn't want to be! Let's just say that, like all women, she *felt the urge*, although not in the same obsessive way as Rosy.She immediately tried to get rid of those erotic thoughts that hovered in her ear like gnats on summer nights and shook her head to shake them off. Then the angels released her, and she advanced to the door they had indicated.

At one point, halfway through, she thought it was strange not to have heard the metal detector. Turning around, she saw Naomi already at the first appointment dispenser touching the screen and the angels urging Rosy to pass through the detector, who seemed to be refusing to do so in order not to lose Hannibal. Almost at the door, though, Martha heard the bell and then Rosy's heart-rending scream, as if the nurse who had helped her give birth in the hospital had taken the baby from her and was selling it to some child trafficker in front of her eyes while she was bedridden and could do nothing but shriek in desperate anguish.

"NOOOOOOOOOOOOOOOO!!! NOOOOOOOOOOOOOOOO!!!! Hannibal NOOOOOOOO!!!!" Rosy had thrown herself on the floor, wrapped up like a foetus, protecting her dildo, kicking, and having a rage as big as Eden itself. So much so, that everyone inside the ark had turned around to see the show. Even the administrative staff had stopped working to watch the dramatic show that Rosy had put on like a Shakespeare play. As for the angels, they had to go for reinforcement.

Martha finally reached the door. She opened it and went through to the other side. She found a huge church with several people kneeling in the pews praying, and with the peculiarity that on the sides there was a pile of confessionals, all of them in deep thought, one next to the other; and each one had a number assigned to it. *Number 4*, thought Marta. She looked for number four and that's where she went. She went in. The cubicle was small. She sat down and closed the door. She waited for someone to speak to her...

She waited...

She stepped out of the cubicle and looked to see if she had stepped into the right place. Yes. It was indeed 4.

She went back in and waited...

...

...

She put her eyes next to the crevices that separated her from the place where the priest was supposed to be to confess her. She could see nothing. It was too dark.

She waited...

...

"Hello?" she asked.
No one answered.
She waited...

...

She left the cubicle again. Just then a man came out of confessional number 3 and asked him how he had managed to be attended to. He told her that he just walked in, and they did it right away, that the priest was already there waiting for him.

"There is no one in my confessional, would you know if I could use yours? Is your priest still there?"

"I think he's gone to get a coffee," the man answered.

Martha looked at him with a puzzled look *'For a coffee?!!!'*

The man decoded her face of incoherent bewilderment and answered her:

I think he said he had a 10-minute break. Anyway, I guess you can't take it. They have people assigned to them. When I came in, he named me directly. Father knew my name.

Fucking hell, Martha cursed. Anyway, she was going to confess anyway. Better to do it now.

"Now, will you excuse me? I have to go and say 10 *Our Fathers*, 15 *Hail Marys* and 4 *Glory Be to the Father*."

Martha's eyes widened like fried eggs. Was that what she had to pray to wash away her sins? Wasn't that a bit much? Did Martha even remember all those prayers?

"Very good. Thank you," Martha said politely.

The man bowed and walked away.

Martha went back inside her confessional and waited...

She waited...

...

...

Until she sighed deeply and intensely, tired of waiting so long, and let out a sigh:

"Why the FUCK do we always have to wait so long here!" She gave a sort of slap to one of the inner walls of the confessional.

"Oh, excuse me!" said the priest on the other side suddenly.

Martha suddenly covered her mouth. She had blasphemed just as the priest had appeared.

"I had gone to the bathroom," he excused himself. "I needed... you know... *the second thing*. And let's just say... the plumbing isn't working quite right today. Something I ate yesterday, probably... All right, tell me... Martha, right?"

"Yes, Martha," the woman confirmed. Clearly, the man was right: people were assigned to priests, *but how?*, she wondered.

"Very well, Martha, what brings you here?"

"Well, I don't know... the metal detector sounded and..."

"Forgive me for interrupting," the priest intervened, "but it's not a metal detector. Yes, it looks like one. But it's not. It's a sin detector."

WHAT!!! the woman exclaimed to herself. She sighed again deeeeeeeply, DEEEEEEEEEEEEPLY, but honestly through her nostrils.

She wanted to explode in a rage. Nevertheless, she held it in.

"You cannot enter Heaven with sins, you must free yourself from them. The sin detector detects the outstanding sins in your soul. Now, let's proceed..."

"All of them?" said Martha.

"All of them."

"ALL my sins?" repeated Martha more emphatically.

"ALL your sins," stressed the priest.

Martha bit her lips and repeated to herself somewhat exasperatedly *all... all... ALL MY SINS*, to which she exhaled with a mixture of irony, knowing that she should also later confess to the latter since her tone of voice had begun to have a certain satanic influence:

"Nowadays, being Heaven and with so much technology... don't you have a printed list of the sins detected by the sin detector and we could go point by point and close this topic as soon as possible? I'd like to die, NOW!" she exclaimed with absolute disgust *NOW!!!*

"That is what the sin detector does. However, the system is currently not working. I'm sorry... the IT group is working on a fix to speed up the process. This has already been escalated to the manager," said Father.

"Ok..." said the woman, grabbing her forehead, taking a deep breath, holding it in, and then letting it all out to start talking once and for all. It really didn't fit in her head what kind of organisation and bureaucracy existed in Heaven, nor did she want to know if the priest was alive or dead, if he worked for the Vatican or if he was a student if the confessions were part of an exam they were taking if they were writing their graduation thesis based on the statements of impurities they heard... Martha was already EX-HAUS-TED. She wanted peace. She wanted PEACE. She wanted P-E-A-C-E. PEACE.

From beginning to end, Martha finally went through all the sins she remembered. She didn't know if they were all of them, but she tried to get rid of a good part of them. She had already notoriously lost track of time since she had entered the tunnel, as there was not a single clock anywhere indicating what time it was.

She measured duration in lumped quantities of her physical, mental, and emotional perception of it based on her experience of being alive. The new definitions of time discriminated between two broad groups: a short time and a long time. The length of the confession with the priest, however, made her hesitate to add a new label beyond a lot, though not as comparable to Prajna's tunnel.

And now, it was time to pay for the cleaning of the confessions... Martha knew it wouldn't be cheap and they had no promotion or discount. So, she would have to repeat who knows how many times the same prayers over and over again. Unless she tried to persuade the priest... though Martha quickly dismissed that thought from her mind, as it would mean a new confession and a price increase. *Do not persuade. Do not persuade*, she repeated to herself.

"100 *Our Father*, 115 *Hail Mary* and 215 *Glory Be to the Father*"

"WHAT THE HELL?!!!!!!!!!!!" she cried out to heaven, even though she was already there. She wanted to kill the priest.

But the priest laughed.

"I was joking, woman. 5 *Our Father*, 4 *Hail Mary's* and 1 *Glory Be to the Father*."

"Now, please!" She put a hand on her chest and felt her heart beating again, "Do you want me to die again? Thank you, Father," she said and put her hand on the little door to push it open and walk out.

"Wait! Before you go, I need to ask you a question."

Marta placed her ass back on the confessional seat. She listened attentively.

"If the man has both God and the Devil," he began the question philosophically, "that is if the man is both God and Devil, don't you think that God is at the same time Devil and the Devil is at the same time God?."

Marta was thinking.

"Don't you think that they are the same entity but that at some point they were separated?" Although he hastened to say, "Don't answer me that!" He almost interrupted himself. "I'll let you get away with that to think…"

Martha came out of the confessional a little confused. The truth was that the question had disconcerted her a little. But now was not the time to philosophise. She wanted to get to the Garden as soon as possible so she could rest, so she set about praying.

When she finished, she went out the door and proceeded to the appointment dispenser and pressed the only button there was to press. The machine issued the ticket under the screen like one child mockingly sticking his tongue out at another and Martha gave it a little pull. She tore it off. It had the number 8923748923467128412846398984789347.

Martha took another deep breath. She couldn't understand why the system didn't restart from the number 100 or 200, or maybe 500; even 1000 she could understand! But the machine counting all the dead people?! It wasn't possible! *The administration must do something about this!*, she thought. So, she folded the ticket in such a way that only 347 was reflected: the last three digits, why else?!

Martha quickly spotted Naomi sitting over there and went to meet her. She sat down next to her and told her about what had happened in the confessional. She also asked about Rosy. Naomi told her that more guards had arrived and that she had been taken down one of the corridors by force, she pointed to the corridor where she had been taken - and that she had never seen her again.

"Ah! Look! There she is!" Noemí pointed with a quick nod of her chin towards the same corridor.

Martha turned around.

Rosy was 'tormented', wrapped like a strudel in a sack of force. Two guards accompanied her, one on each side. Her head was bowed and the lower eyelid of one of her eyes flickered weakly. She walked as calmly as a sloth after a meal. The guards asked her a question in her ear. She raised her hand and pointed to Martha and Naomi. They immediately turned their heads away, pretending not to know her. However, the guards left her there, so they sat her down next to them. Her eye twitched much more than it looked from a distance, while part of her mouth also stretched and returned to normal, absorbed in a hysterical twitch.

"How are you feeling, Rosy?" asked Naomi.

"And... more or less..." she answered, looking at a fixed point on the floor.

"What happened with Hannibal?" asked Martha.

"Hannibal? Who is Hannibal?"

Martha and Naomi looked at each other and that said it all. Their eyes were as wide as the light rings their granddaughters had bought to record themselves on TikTok.

"Ah, yes, Hannibal!" said Rosy suddenly. "It's gone. Hannibal is gone." And she kept repeating softly, in imperceptible murmurs, as she swayed slowly-: "It's gone... It's gone... It's gone... It's... It's... It's gone... It's... It's... It's... gone... "

The other two women understood that it would be better not to bring up the subject of Hannibal.

"And what did they do to you?" asked Naomi.

Rosy suddenly turned her head like those puppets in horror movies and let out a giggle that, rather than funny, was macabre and terrifying. Her voice did not arouse fear, but the expression on her face did.

"I don't know... they put something in me to calm me down," she said with a smile. "They said it was holy water," she added. "Pure as the Virgin Mary I am now."

Martha and Naomi returned an affirmative, though somewhat forced, smile. Not because they did not believe her. She was evidently calm, but because the situation was rather awkward, it was unnecessary to add to her remark about being as pure as the Virgin. Then Rosy returned her gaze to the previously fixed point and said no more words. Martha and Naomi looked at each other again. Neither added anything more. They straightened their shoulders and settled into their seats to wait their turn. The monitors showed 892374892346712841284639898789200. Martha's appointment ended in 347. *UGH!!!*, she complained.

Part 4

Naomi went through first, as she had got her turn earlier. Martha wondered why Naomi hadn't heard the buzzer sound when she passed through the detector. She looked back to the area where the queue was. She saw that not everyone had been beeped at the buzzer. In fact, she hadn't heard it go off for quite some time. It couldn't be true that they all got to Heaven without sin. Something had to be wrong. Well, to tell the truth, several things in Heaven were not working at all well! It wasn't all *PERFECT*, as they had been made to believe on Earth. The bureaucratic side of things was as cumbersome, if not more so, than in the world of the living, she had come to think.

She looked to the side and there was still Rosy muttering under her breath, swaying weakly back and forth and with that twitch in her eye. Martha asked her if she was feeling better. She knew it wasn't a very helpful question, but it was a bit of an icebreaker in the silence; Rosy hadn't spoken since she had told them she had been injected with holy water. Rosy responded with a fragile yes and nothing more.

The monitor was already showing the number ending in 340. There were only 7 left for her to be called. However, as 340 moved to second place, 355 appeared first with the indication to approach booth 2. Martha looked at her turn. She looked at the screen again. She looked around in confusion. Fourteen numbers had been skipped: from 341 to 354. She saw other heads bobbing up as surprised as she was and looking for their corresponding concerned and worried colleagues.

As Martha turned her head to the side, she saw a scrawny nun approaching the boxes. She noticed that the rest of the 13 heads also turned towards her. The woman shuffled her feet, taking very short steps. She accompanied her gait with the movement of her arms as if she were running a marathon.

She was smiling wide at the tremendous wrinkles that weighed her down; you could tell that the risorius muscle lay lifting more weight than her quads and buttocks at once. She was so short that Martha remembered the breakfast bar in her kitchen; the lady would simply take a head off her. Time had worn down her bones and dehydrated her intervertebral discs so that her normal stature had been greatly reduced in the last 20 years, and the woman was well over a century old!

The woman looked this way and that looking to find which booth to go to. She did not know that 56 fangs were lurking behind her in case she went to the boxes marked between 1 and 10 since on the monitors the only number less than 10 was 2.

Marta looked to the side and could see a group of women all dressed alike sitting in a corner separated from the rest. She stood up to get a better view. She focused with a furrowed brow. Yes, she had seen well. They were nuns. She didn't know if it had happened suddenly or if they had been there before and she hadn't noticed, but a group of nuns were in a kind of VIP area also waiting to be served.

Then another number appeared on the screens... it ended in 403. And a nun, almost 50 years younger than the previous one, who had not yet located cubicle number 2, got up and went to her colleague. She directed her to booth 2, and then she went to the one she had been assigned to.

Immediately a crowd of people stood up and began to protest. Several guardian angels approached to keep order. The nuns in the VIP area turned a blind eye. The lady sitting to Martha's right came up to her ear and pointed in gossip mode:

"Weren't we all the same in God's eyes after all?" Her legs were crossed, and the foot that was left dangling was nervously moving in all directions. Her arms were crossed, too, she said, "and look at them playing the dead gnats! They don't say *a* word!"

Martha preferred not to give her opinion. She simply listened to her and nodded her head, some gesture of her mouth or some noise like *mmm...* or *aha...*

"They keep quiet over there to be first," the woman continued. "They should be the first to cede their place. They have no mercy for those of us who are waiting here for our turn. It's unfair!" Then she stood up and, shaking her fist in the air, she repeated loudly: "IT'S UNFAIR!" and she immediately joined the chorus of the others: "UNJUSTICE! UNJUSTICE!"

Immediately a guardian angel approached her and tried to calm her down. At that moment, a powerful voice called for silence through the loudspeakers. Martha guessed it was God. She didn't know his voice, but she perceived it. Or maybe it was the ark manager, who knows? Nevertheless, Martha had the impression that it was more God than any other being. Her skin had gone goosebumps and the hair on her arm stood up like a meerkat on the lookout for danger. It was as if her own father, the one who had begotten her, had raised his voice at her for messing up her room. She was afraid. And she assumed that all the people there felt the same as she did. That's why she also thought it was God.

Martha then found herself perplexed, astonished at the volatile bipolarity of the voice. Immediately after such a shout to calm them all down, the voice subsided in the blink of an eye to politely indicate that he understood the disappointment but that the nuns had been in the service of the Lord all their lives and that it was reasonable to give them priority; to please calm down and return to their seats, and that the allocation of appointments would be resumed in the manner that after two people were appointed from the VIP area, they would continue with two from the general waiting room; then two from the VIP; two from the general, two from the VIP, two from the general. And so on until there was no one else in the VIP and then it would continue as normal. Everyone agreed and returned to their seats.

Finally, the number 347 appeared on the screens and Martha made her way to the designated box. As she got up from her chair, she greeted Rosy and told her that she would see her later in the garden. Rosy looked up and smiled as best she could.

The box was basically like the immigration sector in airports: a small square human fishbowl where the person who received your passport sat and took your fingerprint. Such a fishbowl had a narrow space attached to a narrow board that served as a document holder at a height where both the sender standing and the receiver sitting in the fishbowl could manoeuvre the papers back and forth. Just above the opening was a circular device that served both as a microphone and a loudspeaker. And if everything was correct and approved, a narrow corridor led the traveller directly to Duty-Free.

In the box that Martha had been assigned, a woman with bushy white hair and glasses that stretched sideways like elf ears was waiting for her. Her lips were painted a strong red, her cheeks a shy pink and her eyelids a shiny platinum blue, like a typical secretary, at least her make-up was pretty basic, like when you get a secretarial job and you have no fucking idea how to do your make-up and that's the first thing you try; and Marta saw herself reflected in her since she had been a secretary in the 80s and did her make-up just like that lady! Her brown eyes were so big they looked as if they were about to pop out of their sockets like a Chihuahua dog, and one of them had a slight deviation.

Marta approached with a smile and greeted the microphone cordially. The lady on the other side of the glass did not answer. She silently gave her a quick sidelong glance and returned her pupils to the monitor. With her fingers ready on the keyboard, she asked in a listless, guttural, chain-smoking voice:

"Name?"

"Martha."

"Complete," she ordered, killing her with another sidelong glance. This time, however, she didn't take it away. She held it until Martha answered her request.

"Marta Victoria Herrera."

"Year of birth?"

Martha told her the year and the woman pressed the *enter* key of the number command with her right index finger.

"Where are you travelling to?"

"Where am I travelling to?" Martha was surprised. They were all going to the same destination, *weren't they*, she frowned.

"Where are you going?" she repeated, glaring at her out of the corner of his eye.

"To Heaven?" She hesitated... Unless she was being diverted to Hell.

The lady snorted, removing her glasses, and rubbing her eyes with her left thumb and forefinger.

"Where in Heaven, Martha?"

Marta felt a certain fear. The woman's voice was horrifying and her attitude terrifying.

"Well, I don't know."

"Didn't they give you a piece of paper at the entrance of the tunnel?"

"No, they didn't."

"Who attended to you?" she said, sighing deeply again and demonstrating her experience in the field. It was obvious that she had been working in the migration part of Heaven for a very looooooong time if that's what you could call it, and she was sick and tired of having the most novice people in the first part of the customer service.

"A little guy. I don't know his name."

"This is what you get for employing students!' She angrily said to herself, shaking her head 'I have to do everything twice as much now!" Then she stretched her hand over the document holder towards the opening of the fish tank and asked Marta: "Let me have the passport, please."

Marta was stunned.

"Passport?"

"Are you deaf?" The woman faced her and stared at her.

Martha had never felt such fear, or more than fear, such intensity in her gaze, as she could see how frighteningly the averted eyes exerted an abysmal force, trying to align themselves to seek the fixity and solidity of Martha's gaze; and it was chilling. Marta's skin crawled with goosebumps.

"I beg your pardon?" Marta confronted her.

"Are you deaf? The passport! It's simple: if you don't present the documents that are given to you once you're dead, you must give me the passport!"

"What passport are you talking about?" Marta didn't back down, accompanying it with an Italian gesture with her left hand. She also raised the tone of her voice. She then noticed that two guardian angels were approaching her, one on either side, blocking her way to wherever she wanted to escape. However, Martha had no desire at any point to escape; as always, she was going to fight to her full strength.

She was exhausted. Already her patience had reached demonic levels and her tongue would at any moment dress into a Mephistophelian creature: she would still be fine, refined, but wicked and all out. She would not be silent. She pointed at the guardian angels creeping towards her and threatened them, "Don't you dare come any nearer, or I'll turn you into fallen angels!"

The guardian angels were perplexed and went no further. All the people in the ark had set their eyes on Martha, either discreetly or indiscreetly. However, she was not interested. On the contrary, it was time to call attention to herself in some way. Since she had died, everything had gone wrong, wrong, wrong…

Martha looked at the woman again and faced her with a powerful gaze. She saw that she had a little sign with her name on it hanging on her chest. She said to her:

"Look," she read, "Antonia! I've had enough trouble since I died! You have two options: you let me pass, or you let me pass!.."

"PASSPORT!" she demanded, tapping the tip of her right index finger on the document holder with each syllable uttered.

Martha hit the glass separating them with both hands. Antonia, however, didn't even flinch. She barely blinked. She had such a stubborn personality that she could lead a fly to its tiredness. Antonia was well suited to pester flies around a piece of dung until they moved to another, already annoyed by her presence. And the fact was that she would force them to migrate to another piece of dung located more than 5 kilometres away, because if they did so to one within that distance, Antonia would go and keep harassing them. She was consistent in her decisions and feelings. She was immovable.

"Do you know that you are so annoying that Munch painted *The Scream* as a self-portrait after having argued with you?" Martha blurted out with that graceful palate she had for insults. Well, what they called her tongue when she got furious: the Mephistophelian tongue. She went on describing the picture in front of Antonia's irritated gaze: "Those hands holding poor Munch's face, which was melting from the heat YOU were causing in his ears after having to listen to you in your stubbornness."

"PASSPORT!" repeated the woman, raising her voice even higher and hitting the document holder even harder.

"HOW DO YOU WANT ME TO BRING MY PASSPORT TO HEAVEN? WHO HAS THEIR PASSPORT IN HERE, EH, EH, EH! DOES EVERYBODY DIE WITH THEIR PASSPORT IN THEIR POCKET?" she looked around for someone who was showing their passport. Clearly, there was no one, or at least she couldn't see them. "AND YOU STAY WHERE YOU ARE!" she immediately turned to the angels, pointing at them with consistency. A few more of them had approached. "IF YOU COME CLOSER, I'LL STICK THOSE FLOATING HALOES ON YOUR HEADS WHEREVER YOU AT LEAST EXPECT THEM TO GO!" She threatened them angrily and saw several of them take a few steps backwards.

Then she turned back to Antonia, closed her eyes, took a deep breath in through her nose while biting her lips, then released the air through her mouth and opened her eyes. She faced her pupils straight at her like a Viking arrow to the chest. She spoke softly through her teeth, pretending to have regained some of her composure, "Look, lady, I don't have a passport and I don't see anyone who does. Is there any other way you can let me into my eternal rest? There's a phone there," she said with a quick glance at the side of the computer and turned her pupils to the woman. "Can you pick it up, dial the appropriate intern number, get in touch with the guy who's doing the internship and ask him to e-mail you my documents? It's a question of will, I think."

"Passport," repeated Antonia, albeit with a smile and an ironic air.

"Well, can't you say anything else?" she laughed and continued ironically: "Very well, understanding that you are as square as a Picasso painting?"

"Madam!" said the employee in the cabin with her back to Antonia when she saw that Martha was about to burst out again. She had not managed to hear what she was saying to her stubborn companion, but she had read her lips, so she took the opportunity to answer: "Unfortunately the systems are not working well lately between Earth and Heaven. The people working from the Vatican at the entrance to the tunnels are working with a direct connection to them. We are working on service improvement."

"What should I do then?" Marta asked the woman through the glass.

"Passport," she heard Antonia saying.

She gave her a quick look of contempt.

"You must go back to the beginning of the tunnel and ask for the document."

"HOW?!" She exclaimed in astonishment, *ALL THE DAMN ETERNAL WAY AGAIN?!!!!*

"Yes, all over again"' the woman replied in sorrow.

Martha had forgotten that everything she thought was as open as saying it out loud in front of the employees. They had the right to hear everything. There was no such thing as privacy. In the Kingdom of God, everything was known.

"But I don't see anyone who has any paper," insisted Martha.

"It's just that it's not a paper in physical format. They will tell you a number. That number corresponds to your file. You must come with that number and tell us."

Martha sighed again.

"I'm sorry..." said the woman, grimacing with her mouth, bitter that she had to break the news to her.

"I thank you," Martha replied with a smile, albeit with a rather sour tinge. Then she turned to look Antonia up and down. "As for you..." she laughed softly, raised her chin, and with noble pride, added, "How much you could do with a Hannibal!" She turned and walked away, making her way through the guardian angels.

It was the only moment when Antonia's face changed from that of a bitter, badly painted bulldog to a face of *What did she mean by Hannibal!* She sat back down in front of the monitor and called the next number on the list.

Part 5

Martha passed through the sin detector again after turning back towards the tunnel. It beeped until it almost exploded. It made so much noise and emitted so many coloured lights that smoke began to come out of the cracks. Martha had undoubtedly thought more profanities in those moments with Antonia than she had sinned in her entire life.

The people in the queue were upset with Martha for having broken the detector, as they would now have to wait longer for it to be repaired or replaced. However, the woman did not make a big deal out of it. What she did do was, before exiting the ark, stop, turn, and say loudly for all to hear as she made huge circles in the air with her arm and forefinger, unperturbed and consistent, above her head in an exaggerated way to make it understand that she was speaking to EVERYONE, ABSOLUTELY EVERYBODYYYYYYYYY in the ark:

"AND I WANT YOU TO KNOW THAT I HAVE ALREADY DONE ALL THIS FUCKING STUFF, AND THAT WHEN I COME BACK WITH MY FUCKING DOCUMENT, WHICH HEAVEN ITSELF FORGOT TO GIVE ME, GIVE ME A *FUCKING* SEAT" she pronounced fucking so strongly in her consonants that while some nuns in the VIP covered their mouths, others bowed their heads and made the sign of the cross "IN THE NUNS VIP SPACE!" she finished by marking with her arm the corner where the nuns lay waiting for their turn "THANK YOU!" she finally spat and left the ark.

Everyone looked at her in bewilderment. Even though she had spoken to those in the ark, she assumed that her shriek had reached the end of the tunnel. She heard many in the line say that she was insensitive, impudent, insolent, that she deserved to go to Hell, that she was a heathen, how could she talk like that... They whispered among themselves about her attitude or gave her a grudging look as she passed, and some even said it to her face. Martha, however, laughed in their faces without giving them the slightest credit.

She arrived at the tunnel and there was the bellboy who had welcomed her, Naomi and Rosy. She greeted him. The bellboy tried to stop her as she was going into one of the tunnels, but Martha didn't react. She continued walking down the tunnel as if nothing had happened.

"Madam, you can't go into the tunnel! That's not yours!"

"I don't care three shifts, bellboy!" she exclaimed bluntly and without looking back.

Haughty, taking everything in her stride, laughing... she walked down who knows whose tunnel. She walked with such a firm and emboldened step, like an ox in the heat with blinkers on, that the speed of the conveyor belt could not keep up with her progress. Incidentally, not much further along the tunnel, he found a small metal box the size of a teacup on the side of the conveyor belt. It had two buttons: one green and one red. Martha assumed that the red one would be to stop the conveyor belt, so it would be much easier to walk on it if she did so. However, she didn't. No, she didn't. She had a better idea... Angry as she was, she took some running and gave it a tremendous kick that sent it into the air. She felt like a footballer kicking a penalty kick in the final of some World Cup with a tremendous yearning to punch a hole in the net behind the goal. It was... A-MA-ZING. She had never felt so much happiness in her soul. And noticeably the conveyor belt stopped! She laughed. And LAUGHED with a macabre air of satisfaction.

She did not even look at the person's memories. She went on, went on, went on. She came across the person in a certain part of the tunnel, but she didn't think anything of it. She reached the beginning of the tunnel and saw the old dial telephone. The only thing she could think to dial was 911... who knows, maybe they were answering! Being the only connection to Earth there was, she supposed... However, before they picked up, she hung up. She had noticed something that had caught her attention.

In the black, impenetrable darkness at the start of the tunnel, Martha had detected something. She approached it, stepping into the lushness of the shadows there and noticing a tremendous, calamitous drop in temperature... She reached out with her hands and touched something. She grasped some kind of handle. It was a doorknob. In the darkness at the beginning of the tunnel, a door was hidden. She opened it...

When she opened her eyes, she was lying on her back staring at a hideous, tasteless ceiling. A strong smell of stale wood penetrated her pits as easily as needles into the skin. Her hands were on her sternum, the left hand cupping the right, and between them, they clasped an ethereal bouquet of...

"CALLAS!" she howled in terror and rage and sat upright.

Everyone around her screamed in horror; some fainted, a few ran away, and others were stunned, some of them covering their mouths or not. Martha didn't know how long she had been in Heaven, the last thing she remembered from when she had been alive was in the hospital ward. But certainly, the times up there were different from those down here, for now, she had woken up at her funeral.

"I hate callas! They're for the dead, damn it!" she exclaimed, throwing them on the floor in fury as she tried to get out of the coffin. "And this dress they put me on!" she complained, looking up and down as she removed her other leg from the coffin- "Is this how they were going to make a wake for me?" She made a nauseous face "Who chose it?" she asked, pointing to her daughters, who stood there, motionless, huddled in a corner, terrified. "What's the matter with them? They look like they've seen a ghost!" she laughed. She turned and looked at the coffin.

She felt the smell of stale wood super tight in her nostrils again; Martha thought her senses had probably been further sensitised by her return from the dead. "This is what you spent money on?" she asked in disgust, turning her head and watching her daughters out of the corner of her eye. Then she turned to them while gesturing with her hands, "Please! Pine? And of poor quality? Daughters, please, either pay for something *GOOD*, a minimum of oak, I don't ask for ebony; or else bury me like this, in these creepy pyjamas they put me on, at the back of the house."

Martha's daughters looked at each other. They said nothing. They could not even utter a word. Their faces were still as white as coconut milk and their gestures were so uncoordinated that their brains seemed to have short-circuited.

"Oh, and you're giving me back my little things!" The woman clarified, remembering what she had overheard in the conversation they had had regarding the distribution of her belongings.

A short lady who was with the women, separated from the group with a half-formed smile on her face. It was a hesitant smile that she could not bring herself to smile because she was afraid that what she was seeing was not true; until she asked, being the only one among all those left in the room who dared to discover the truth of what was going on:

"Martha?"

"Yes, Andrea. It's me."

Andrea was Martha's best friend. She had been there in the good times but even more in the bad ones. She was a faithful, humble woman with a big heart. She loved pizza and beer, as well as a good seafood paella by the sea with a glass of red wine. She loved chats and company until dusk fell at midnight with no notion of the cosmos and its metaphysical law of time. Andrea was the non-biological sister; the one Martha had chosen. And as Martha would have guessed, she was the only one at the wake who was not dressed in black, but in red, Martha's favourite colour. And when Martha answered her, Andrea's smile decided to break into a smile, and she began to walk towards her friend.

"Like Christ, resurrected!" Andrea laughed, squeezing her arms with both hands and looking into her eyes.

"Mmm... let's say..." Martha joined her friend's laughter and they embraced, 'Do you want to go for a beer? I feel like having a beer!' she remarked happily.

"I'd like a pizza, too!" added her friend.

Martha agreed.

They walked together down the central aisle to the astonished looks of everyone. When they reached the place where their daughters were standing, they stopped, and Martha turned towards them to approach and greet them. However, at the paltry gesture of executing the first step, the four women shyly stepped back. They still could not get over their shock, but Martha did not restrain her anger at their ridiculous reaction:

"They can all go to Heaven!"

"*To Heaven?*" Andrea wondered aloud and immediately turned to Martha: "*Wouldn't it be to Hell?*"

"No!" she answered almost interposing herself with her eyes about to pop out of their sockets, and continued to stare steadily at her friend, "Believe me!" she nodded her head and moved her right hand downwards as if setting a post in the ground. Her affirmation was immovable, more so than Antonia's stubbornness. "I know why I say it!"

Finally, they left the funeral home, happily discussing which pizza shop they would go to Martha could imagine the smell of Italian tomatoes coming out of the oven. Martha enjoyed the freshness of the wind and the sunlight on her face as never before; the rustle of the leaves and the scent of the grass; the goosebumps on her skin, her feet hopping along the pavement; the company of her friend... It had not only been the smell of wood that she had felt intense, of course not! She had come back to life with her senses enormously heightened. ALL OF THEM.

"And what about it?" Andrea suddenly pulled her out of her world of emotions "Have you seen the tunnel, is it true that it exists?"

"WHEW!" She waved her hand in the air at his shoulder. "Well, you can't even imagine! I've come for my passport..."

Andrea stopped in her tracks and asked her with a confused look on her face:

"Passport...?"

"But I don't really feel like going back... I think I'll stay longer," she smiled at her.

"What are you talking about?" Andrea shook her head and smiled at her, without understanding.

"I'll tell you…" She hugged her, crossing her arm behind her back over his shoulder, and they continued walking to the pizza shop. They would go to Don Raul's.

Printed in Great Britain
by Amazon